Rules and Reputations

THE AFFAIRS OF LOVE AND COURT
BOOK TWO

JENEVIEVE HERNANDEZ

AMETHYST INK PUBLISHING LLC

authorjenevievehernandez.com

Book Cover by Jillian Elyzabeth @jillianelyzstudio

ISBN ebook: 978-1-965713-04-4

ISBN paperback: 978-1-965713-05-1

For my Dad.
Thank you for being the best example of a selfless, kind, and
loving father. I love you!

CHAPTER 1

Santiago

You have *got* to be kidding me. As this thought runs through my mind, I storm out of the door and quickly walk to the garage to get my car. Sliding into the driver's seat, I press the automatic open button for both the garage and gate. I try to picture all of the scenarios that could be putting me in this position, and admittedly, there's a lot.

The glowing lights on my car screen read ten-thirty, and I breathe a sigh of relief because it's still an "acceptable" hour to be out and about. At least Mother and Father won't have an opportunity to breathe down my neck about being out too late. One of the many *lovely* perks of being Santiago Alvarez. Though, in recent months, they've become less strict with me, as though they've given up on fixing me.

My phone rings, cutting off my stream of thoughts, and I glance over to the car screen where it reads "Damon" in glowing letters.

"Hello?"

"Hey, man, when are you going to get here? We're waiting, and you-know-who is...impatient."

I scoff, pressing down on the gas pedal even harder. "Well, tell him that I'm going as fast as the speed limit allows and that he can wait."

"Santi-"

"Damon, just tell him that I'm on my way. There's no reason for him to be so impatient. It's not like I have anywhere else to be. I'll get there when I get there."

"You said that last-"

"That was once," I say, cutting him off before he can finish his sentence. Okay, maybe it's been more than once that I've forgotten about my commitments, but sue me for losing track of time here and there. To be fair, there might be a few instances where I've intentionally left people hanging when I previously let them know that I would be there, so that doesn't necessarily count as being forgetful.

"Yeah, believe what you want to, man. It's not me you're trying to convince. Just get here and get him calmed down he's *not* happy that you're late." Damon finally says, sounding a little bit more than stressed.

"He's never happy. I'm on my way, though. Tell him to stop fretting, and that he can rest assured that I'll be there." I say, my tone more annoyed than before. Clicking the button to end the call, I drop my phone into the passenger seat, not allowing Damon to keep talking. It's not that I *want* to be this rude, but I would much rather be doing this instead of dealing with his talking for the rest of the drive. I'm only five minutes away from The Enchanted Ivy now, and there's no reason to carry a conversation with him anymore.

The security cameras on the gates scan over my car, and they flash green as they accept my license plate, the large gates swinging open for me. Tapping my fingers against the wheel in tune with the bass that's filling my car with a vibration strong enough to shake the water that's in my cupholder, I roll up the elaborate path to the main parking area. The winding road glows in the beam of my headlights, and I suck a breath in before parking next to all of my friends' cars. My eyes glance over each of their vehicles but don't linger, because I know that all of theirs pale in comparison when parked next to mine. Yes, that sounds harsh, but it's simply the truth.

My seventeenth birthday present was better than my eighteenth—which was just a few months ago—in the sense that this one gets much more use. I don't dislike the shares in the Korean business—was it phones? Maybe cars?—that my parents bought me, but those aren't nearly as fun. I much prefer the excitement of driving my car to wherever I please, rather than watching screens with graphs that display hundreds of numbers and dollar signs. One can only look at the dollar number that comes with the shares, not slide behind the wheel and press the gas pedal as the lights of the night fly by. Maybe it was their way of trying to push me into the business world, or maybe it was simply the only gift they could think of. Either way, there's no more time to ponder the meaning behind it, because Damon is approaching me with the stressed look that he only wears whenever Lyle is around.

Lyle has a way of stressing Damon that no one else can pull off. Maybe it's the fact that Damon is the youngest of us and Lyle is the oldest, or the fact that—in the nicest way possible—Damon is at the bottom of the food chain in our group, with myself being at the top.

"What's he all worked up about?" I question as Damon reaches out to slap my shoulder.

"Apparently, he's not too happy about you being late, so our little golfing tournament isn't going to be too pleasant."

"Why not?" Surely Lyle isn't *that* mad about me being late and skipping a few hangouts, right?

"You'll see." Is all Damon says, falling into step with me as we make our way onto the golf course.

"So you finally decided to leave your mansion and join the rest of us?" Lyle calls out when we near, his figure visible under the lights that line the concrete path of the court.

"Something like that. What's up?" I question, straightening as I stop, intentionally looking down at him as I speak. Matteo has told me to stop doing it, something about trying to intimidate people the wrong way, but I see no problem with it. Especially if it's someone like Lyle.

"You think you're so special, only coming to hang with the rest of us when you feel like it, huh?" Lyle essentially sneers.

"No, that's not exactly true. Some of us have other commitments, you know?" I take a breath. "And some of us run much bigger operations," I say, reminding him that while he comes from money, I have a lot more at stake than he does. Us Alvarez are easily at the top of the pyramid, with a few other families at the same level. Not Lyle's, but the Valentino's for sure. Shuddering as the name passes my mind, I bring my thoughts back to the current conversation.

"What, so just because you come from-"

"Don't." I say, reminding him that just because he hasn't

been around me in a while, doesn't mean he gets to slander my name whenever he feels like it.

"Whatever. You're late to the party, so you didn't get a vote on the rules. Loser pays for tomorrow night." Lyle says, a bite in his words.

"Tomorrow night?" I question.

"We're all going coming back here—the club—and having a party."

"But won't the club just handle all of that?"

"If it were a club party, yes. But this is private. We're inviting all of the important people, so just be there." Lyle says, stepping back to where the rest of our friends are gathered. "Oh, and I wouldn't want to lose."

CHAPTER 2
Santiago

The game of golf—night golf at that—is long, and by the time we're nearing the end, I almost would rather lose, if only to leave early. It feels like I can already see the coral coloring of the morning sun, although sunrise is still not for another few hours.

After swinging, I can tell that my ball went in the right direction and should be near enough to the hole that I'll just need one putt.

Another thirty minutes pass, and as Lyle and a few of the other guys tally up the scores, a shiver rolls down my body as the wind gusts again. I twist my wrist to glance down at my gold watch, and I'm not surprised that it's one-forty-five in the morning. At this point, I'd rather just leave and pay for tomorrow night rather than stand out here with nothing to do. I'm not even sure why I agreed to this stupid challenge, but it's not going to harm my bank account either way. Maybe it's just for the thrill of having something at stake and then winning.

"And the loser is..." Lyle drags out the announcement, intentionally causing groans and huff throughout our group. "Stiles."

"Aw, man, seriously? Whatever. I'm out of here." Stiles grumbles, brushing past me on his way out.

"Sore loser, huh?" Lyle says, trying to bring the attention back to himself. "It doesn't matter, though. At least I'm not the one paying for tomorrow."

"Yeah-"

"You never announced the winner," I interject, stepping closer to the group, interrupting Martin, and cutting my glance to Lyle.

"Oh, yeah. I guess I did. Sorry about that." Lyle says, turning his eyes down to the score sheet he's been keeping, as though he can't remember who won.

"Well?" I prod.

"The winner was Santiago. Yay." Lyle admits, his false enthusiasm humorous. The jealousy is obvious in his voice, and I can't help but allow a smirk to play across my face.

"Thank you, everyone. Now that I've won, I think I'll be heading back to my place. Have a good night." I say, tipping my imaginary hat at everyone before turning.

Another win in the books, and another party later today. I'd expect nothing less from the life of Santiago Alvarez.

"Where have you been, Santi?" A voice calls out from behind the slightly-opened bedroom door. Matteo is still awake. Perfect. "I'm not deaf, you know? When you walk loudly through the hall, it's hard to not notice that you're home."

"Oh my gosh, I'm coming," I say, pushing open his bedroom door. At this point why doesn't he speak a little bit louder and wake up Carmen?

"Well?" He says from his sofa near the back of his room. I stride towards him, flopping down on his bed before responding.

"I was golfing with the guys," I say rolling over to face the ceiling of his room. It still has a few of the glow-in-the-dark stars and moon stickers that he hung at seven years old. They're barely visible with the lamp light on, but I still focus on them, their greenish tint fascinating.

"Why? I thought you were having a hard time with all of them or something?" Matteo asks, his eyes not lifting from the novel in his hand. Knowing Matteo, it's probably some business book that he'll read and actually try to understand.

"Or something. I never told you what was happening, you know?" I remind him, not liking how much he knows about my personal life.

"Whatever, Santiago." My skin pricks as his words slice through the air. There used to be a time when I would immediately listen to him whenever he showed disapproval, and while I don't outwardly show it now, I still feel that automatic want to earn his approval.

Ugh. Outwardly scoffing at my thoughts, I push myself off of Matteo's bed and stride towards the door. "Did you need me for anything else? Other than poke into my personal life, that is?"

"Nope." Matteo answers, his eyes never leaving the book in his hands.

Walking into my room, I quickly shower and change into sweatpants and a cotton shirt, crawling into my unmade bed. All of the teasing and snide remarks that Lyle made while we were golfing are still weighing on me, and the longer I think about them, the angrier I become.

I took time out of my night to go golf with his annoying self, and then he spent the whole time irritating me. Thinking back on these past few weeks when I ignored all of his pleas to hang out with the group, the memories of just being alone and not annoyed all of the time flash through my mind. While it wasn't exactly peace, it was still better than tonight.

Maybe it's the validation that people want to spend time with me, or maybe it's the fact that I feel suffocated under my family's scrutinizing gazes, but being around my "friends" is the only escape I have that's not being entirely alone. It really is pathetic, I know.

CHAPTER 3

Santiago

Slipping past Matteo on the stairs, I take the next few multiple stairs at a time, knowing that out of curiosity, he's going to ask where I'm going, and I'd rather be out of earshot before he asks. With me, it's more curiosity. With Carmen, he's downright protective. I'm the same way. Matteo's comings and goings don't really worry me, rather I'm just curious. With Carmen, I'm always worried that she's going to find herself in a dangerous situation.

"Heading out?" My brother calls, just loud enough to where I have to answer.

"Yep. See you later." Taking his silence as an escape opportunity, I skip the last few stairs and move through the house, quietly shutting the front door behind me. The security team is surely watching me, but I'm not too worried. They're well aware of my comings and goings, and they've yet to mention it to my parents as suspicious since there's technically nothing strange about it.

The large garage that houses my car, Matteo's, and

Mother's—which she never drives—is a welcome sight after being in the house all day. I slip into the driver's seat of my car, running my hands over the wheel before starting it, then press the garage door button.

A calm sense of peace settles over me as I drive, the familiar feel of my car relaxing. Images of the past parties that Lyle and the guys have thrown flit throughout my mind, and all of the memories of me being wasted and stupid burn behind my eyes. Maybe I'm not perfect, but I'm not as bad as I once was. I remind myself of this when I roll through the entrance gates to The Enchanted Ivy.

Parking near the front entrance, I pass my keys to one of the many club staff, knowing they'll move it over to their parking. Pushing open the doors, and striding to the main room, the first thing I notice is the sound. Music is blaring loud enough that my head is pounding, but instead of moving away from the noise, I move even deeper into the room.

"Hey, man, you made it," Damon calls out, his voice louder than necessary.

"Yeah, it appears I did. What are you doing?" I reply, as if it's not quite obvious that he's been here since before the party started.

"Just hanging, we've been having a great time, you know?" He says, motioning around him as if I should've mentioned it.

"I gather that. Have fun, man." I say, patting his shoulder and moving across the room. My hand moves through the iced drinks until I find a soda. Again, maybe I'm not perfect—just being here proves that—but I'm not making entirely bad decisions. It's the small wins. An employee looks me up and down as I do this, and I realize that it was her job to distribute the drinks. Instead of apologizing, I give her one of my signature half-smiles and a wink. She looks slightly flustered, and I can tell that she's probably my age, or just a little bit younger.

Leaning against one of the walls, watching my friends and strangers party like there's no tomorrow, I sip the nasty soda that I chose. Why didn't I check the flavor before taking it?

"So you're not much of a party monster, then?" A feminine voice says close to me. I turn to see a *very* pretty girl leaning on the wall next to me, her curly hair framing her face, the dim lights accentuating her light brown skin, the color accentuating her puffy lips, and big eyes perfectly.

"Sorry?" I cough out, feeling flustered by the stunning woman in front of me. She surely can't be older than me, but she's also not younger than Carmen.

"I asked why you aren't partying with all of your friends." She says point blank, lifting an eyebrow at me.

"Because I'm trying to leave the stupid parties like these behind me," I reply, shifting so I can look at her better.

"That's cool, I guess." She says, eyeing the soda in my hand, then lifting her eyes back to mine.

"Yeah," I reply, losing all sense of...anything as I gaze into her dark brown eyes. "Sorry, I missed your name."

"I didn't say it." She says with a smirk, extending her hand. "It's Brooklynn Carmine."

Taking her extended hand, I shake it, her small hand almost slipping out of mine. "Santiago Alvarez."

"I already knew that. Some of your friends are *very* talkative, you know?" Brooklynn says, biting her lip before raising her own drink to her lips. I can tell that it's non-alcoholic, but I'm not sure what it is.

"So, where have I heard your name before? I recognize it." The words roll from my lips and I watch her reaction.

"You probably have heard it. I was in the new romance movie that just released. Our Story. My co-star and I-" She coughs and takes a sip of her drink before finishing. "-are gaining quite the popularity from it. It debuted with a pretty impressive amount of theater viewers." Brooklynn says with a soft smile.

"Wow, that's pretty cool. I knew I'd heard your name before."

"Hey, I have an extra strange question, but do you know that guy over there?" She asks completely changing the topic, pointing across the room to someone hanging out near the corner of the room, not even a drink in hand as he absently watches the other young adults here party.

I swallow a rude remark and remind myself that I'm supposed to be keeping my word. "Yeah, I used to."

"Used to? What's his name? I kind of want to go talk to him." Brooklynn says, a curious look in her eyes.

Go talk to him? As if Alessandro Valentino hasn't done enough to ruin my life, he's—without even trying to—stealing a girl's attention from me. "Why?"

"Why does it matter? I think he's rather nice looking." She says, looking up through her eyelashes when she speaks.

"Because we have history, and it's not very good," I say, hearing the venom in my own words.

"Goodness, Santiago, calm down. You're good-looking, too." Brooklynn says, as though this was only about her saying he looks nice. "You know..." She looks me up and down as if she's considering something as her gaze travels my body.

"You know what?" I finally ask after she doesn't speak, her mind obviously moving a mile a minute.

"I was-" She snaps her mouth shut then clears her throat before talking again. "-I was just thinking that you might be the perfect boyfriend for me."

"*Boyfriend?*" I sputter out, feeling slightly unsure of whatever she's insinuating.

"Yeah, it's kind of complicated, but I really need someone to help me out, and you're good-looking enough to fit the bill," Brooklynn says, her smile growing. "Oh, and don't worry, I'm not interested in you or anything. I'm just *really* in a little pinch right now." She says with a smile that's supposed to look innocent. And if I'm being honest, I might have fallen for it had she not just told me that she wants to use me for some fake dating ruse.

"So I'm supposed to pretend to date you? Is that why you were asking about him?" I ask, gesturing to where Alessandro was standing earlier.

"Of course. Why do you think I'm here with all of these boys? I would much rather be spending time elsewhere, but desperate times call for desperate measures, you know." Brooklynn says, tapping at her phone screen before looking up. "So you're in, then? You're going to help me get out of this little mess I'm in?" She asks, as if realizing I never even agreed to her plan.

"Why exactly do you need a boyfriend again? I think I missed that part." I question, my mind spinning from everything she's saying.

"Oh, honey, I can't tell you that. It's...complicated." Brooklynn says, as if that's reason enough for me to agree.

"What do you need me to do? This isn't my official agreement, though." I'm not even sure why I'm considering this crazy idea that I know nothing about, but for some reason, I have a feeling I won't be able to say no.

"I just need pictures of us together that we can cleverly leak to the public, so it seems as though I have a boyfriend. That way, the attention is on that, and not on...other things." Brooklynn says, snapping a quick photo of our legs and feet, bringing her cell phone screen to my eyes. "Like this. It looks like a date or something, and will totally get people talking. Do you mind if I post this?" She asks, her dark eyes looking up at me with so much hope that I have to agree. What is this girl even doing to me?

"Sure, but what is this going to do to my public image?"

"What public image? Let's not forget who had to be told who you were, when you knew me by just my name." Brooklynn says with a raised eyebrow and a smirk. This girl knows exactly how to make me feel great, and then smack my ego ten seconds later. "But don't worry, no one is going to know who my new mystery man is."

"Okay then. Just, no one can know that I'm the person in these photos. I'm kind of on thin ice with a lot of people, and a relationship with someone like you wouldn't be the best thing for my public appearance right now."

"Someone like me?" Brooklynn asks indignantly, a hand to her chest, clearly horrified.

"I didn't mean that in a bad way. I just meant that there are going to be quite a few people who won't be too happy that I'll be dragging down your status. So, as long as people don't know it's me, we'll be fine." I quickly amend, realizing how I sound.

"What do you mean? What have you done to make people think that?" Brooklynn asks curiously. "Do you mean to tell me that you're a bad boy? This is going to be even better."

"Are you okay?" I ask, not even bothering to answer her question, her excitement over me possibly being a "bad boy" slightly concerning.

"Of course I am. What an insulting question." Brooklynn replies, "You just don't understand how these things work, do you?"

"I just don't understand *you*. Mind you, we've known each other for maybe twenty minutes, and I'm already being used in some elaborate press move." I tease, chuckling as I say the words.

"You might be on to something, but just know that I came to this silly party to scout out good candidates for my master plan. I didn't come looking for you or something." Brooklynn assures me, as though I got the idea that she was seeking me out.

"Trust me, I didn't think so little of you, Brooklynn."

"Perfect. What is the best way to get in contact with you?" Brooklynn asks, handing me her phone, apparently not worried about what I might do with it.

"I guess a message or call? Here, let me add my number to your contacts." Entering my information, a message chimes, and a notification pops up on the screen. Without even a chance to look at it, Brooklynn snatches it from me, her eyes roaming over the screen hurriedly.

"You might just be the best fake boyfriend that I've ever

had. People are already curious about who you are, and if we're dating." Brooklynn says with a smile.

"I'm honored. Hopefully, the best fake boyfriend you've had so far." I reply, not sure of what else to say. I'm probably going to regret all of this in the morning when I'm not under the influence of no sleep and Brooklynn's charming personality, but until then, this is fun. While Brooklynn is undeniably beautiful, I can tell that she's serious about this plan of hers, and I'm definitely not her type.

"I must be going, but this has been fun, Santiago. We're going to get along well. I can already tell." She says with a smile, passing me her barely sipped soda, weaving through the crowds of people towards the exit. Glancing down at the soda she just passed me, I smile. This girl is maybe the most confusing person I've ever met. Most people would say the same of me, so I guess we're the same in that sense. Although, I don't think I would just approach a random girl and ask her to be my fake girlfriend.

CHAPTER 4
Brooklynn

Parties like those always leave a bitter taste in my mouth. I have to hang out with gross boys, act like I care when they drone on and on about things that bore me to death, and never do anything that might ruin the carefully constructed public image that my publicists and I have formed. Well, that we formed and kept up until now. It really is *quite* exhausting.

My private driver hums along to the pop music that softly plays throughout the car speakers, and I glance back down at my phone, the chimes of messages sending a rush through blood.

Has Kai seen the photo, yet? Has the media picked up on it?

These thoughts flit through my mind as I scroll through the messages of people replying to my post. I sigh and close my phone, knowing that I've done enough for now. Tapping my foot impatiently, I wonder just how long small media outlets will take before they run a story on it. Do I need to be more obvious with these photos?

"We're home, Miss Brooklynn, is there anywhere else that you need me to drive you to, tonight?"

"No thank you, Mr. Stone," I say, slipping out of my seat and into the barely chilly air, making my way to the front door of my parents' mansion. It's highly unlikely that they'll be awake, but even still, I'm quiet as I walk to my wing in the house.

"Brooklynn, we've had two new movies that are interested in you, as well as a television series that's been adapted from a book. I think that we need to sit down and discuss them, make no final decisions, but at least just get a feel for where we're at. How does that sound?" My manager, Marie, asks over the phone. "We also need to talk about the Kai situation, as well."

"Yeah, we can work something out. When do you want to meet?" I ask, slightly absently. A message just appeared from Santiago, and I'm curious as to what he has to say.

"Does today work? I think we need to do a deeper dive into what you want to do, and how often you want to work. I mean, you're still seventeen years old, not to mention you're still in school." Marie says, pointing out the obvious.

"I can work something out for today. Do you want to meet at your office?"

"Yes. Does three work for you?"

"Sure. I'll be there then."

"Thank you, Brooklynn. I'll see you later." The line clicks, and Marie's voice is gone. Well, now I have to prepare myself for a meeting today. It's not that I dislike Marie, it's just that I'm still mildly stressed about Kai, and figuring out if he's still not over me. Which is totally crazy, because a few months ago, I wouldn't have thought that this would be an issue in my life.

After quickly doing my makeup and sending a text to my driver, I slide on a cute outfit that consists of a mini denim skirt, a white top, and a leather jacket. Paired with my leather boots, my outfit is adorable, and I have to smile at my ability to put together outfits that I consistently love.

Swinging my purse over my shoulder, I brush past Mom on my way out.

"Honey, where are you off to so quickly?" She asks, her blonde hair in a flawless blowout and her makeup done to perfection. I guess she's off to somewhere, too.

"A meeting with Marie. How about you?" I question, Dad coming to stand next to Mom. His height shadows her, and I'm once again grateful I inherited her shorter size. No offense, Dad, but I'm not built to be six-foot-four. I'll take your curl genes and darker skin, but not the height. That's one of the reasons why I was specifically cast for the role of Macey in Our Story. My height was perfect next to Kai's, with me being five-four, and him being just about six-foot. Although, looking back, maybe not being cast would have been better in the long run.

"We're going to lunch. We were going to ask you to come along, but I guess you already have plans." She says with a smile, taking Dad's large hand in her own.

"When will you be back home?" Dad asks, his deep voice a stark contrast to Mom's light one.

"I don't really know. Marie would like to discuss all of the roles I've been offered, and to go over how much I want to act every year." I say, waving my hand in an unsure gesture.

"But you're not making any final decisions, though? We should probably all discuss how much you'll be working before you officially agree to anything, right?" Mom asks, sounding slightly concerned.

"Oh, yeah, for sure. Marie wants to just see where I'm at. She even said that there are going to be no final decisions done today." I assure my parents, looking over at the wall clock, noticing the time. "I need to get going, but have a nice lunch."

"Thank you. Have a good afternoon, too." Dad calls out from behind me.

Once I'm seated in the back seat of the car, with my driver behind the wheel, I pulled out my phone and check the message Santiago sent me. Technically, I did message him first, but he responded.

My message said that people were reacting to the photo just the way I wanted them to, and that he's already being the perfect fake online boyfriend. I of course made sure to make sure to let him know that it was my good camera angles and not him, but he seems to have skipped that part.

His response says that he's glad it's going the way I want it to, and he wants to know if my family is a member of The Enchanted Ivy country club. It's the same place the party was at last night, but the party I attended was private.

I'll have to ask Dad later today. We just moved in here a

few weeks ago, so I'm not sure if my parents are in all of the social club things, yet. I message a response relaying my thoughts, and he doesn't respond.

"Would you like me to stay here, or come back at a later time?" Mr. Stone asks as he pulls up to Marie's building. Well, technically, it's her company's building, and her office is just in it.

"You're good to leave. I'll give you a call or message when I need you. I think I might be here for a while." I reply with a smile, allowing him to get out and open the door for me.

"Sounds good, ma'am. Have a nice afternoon, and call me when you're in need of another ride." He says, closing the door behind me.

"Thank you."

"It's my pleasure."

Entering the building, the city streets around me bustling, I suck in a breath and remind myself that I'm supposed to be here. Sometimes it feels like Our Story doing well has nothing to do with me, and that at the snap of a finger, my whole world will return to what it was before.

My family has always had money, but it was the fruits of my father's labor. With him being an actor back in his day—occasionally he'll pick up a very large role here and there, but that's rare—I've always had the dream of acting, myself.

Before my thoughts can spiral down to what the critics say about me, Marie is in front of me with open arms.

"Hello, Brooklynn. So lovely of you to have made it over on such short notice." I accept her embrace and give her a quick hug before falling into stride with her.

"It's been a while since I've been here," I comment, noticing a few subtle decor changes.

"July, right?" Marie questions.

"I believe so. Definitely before Our Story premiered." I say, doing the math. "Our Story was two weeks ago, right?"

"Yes. Which, speaking of, is doing wonderful. I know that people are still holding on to that, but that other movie that you filmed last year, Summer's Mirage, is just being teased right now, and people are eating it up." Marie says excitedly.

"Really?" I ask, almost forgetting the movie that I filmed last summer. Funny enough, Kai was also the main male lead, too. His career is a little bit ahead of mine, with his name being big in the young adult category, but after Our Story, I have almost as much social media presence as him. I knew that Summer's Mirage wouldn't be an immediate release—unlike Our Story, which was filmed, edited, and sent out to the world in six months—and that the directors had big plans for it.

"Oh, yes, Brooklynn. It's already looking like it will be *much* bigger than Our Story. I know that with that release there weren't any press conferences, premiers, and so on, but I'm betting that all of that and more will accompany Summer's Mirage." Marie says as we step on the elevator.

"That's really exciting, Marie. To be honest, I kind of forgot that movie even existed." Which is silly, seeing as it was the first movie I'd ever starred in. In my head, Our Story is my first and only movie. I guess that's what happens when you film a movie, and over a year later, you start getting updates on it.

"You've been a pretty busy girl. I don't blame you." Marie says, steering me into her office after we step off of the elevator.

"I like what you did there," I say, gesturing at the pink sofa that is on the far wall.

"Ah, thank you. I rather like it, myself." She moves around her desk, motioning for me to sit in the chair across from her. I do so, moving closer to the desk to look down at all of the papers that cover her desk. "So, I'm first going to explain each of the roles that you've been offered, and then we'll talk about your future in acting, and all of those fun things." Marie explains, waving her hands over the sets of papers.

"Okay, that sounds good. Go ahead." I say with a smile, both excited and nervous about what she has to tell me.

"Perfect. To start, we have two movies and a television show that have already pre-selected you for the role, which means they're offering you the spot without any type of audition. Which, is huge. You've definitely opened the door for so many good opportunities with how well you performed on Our Story."

"Thank you," I say, feeling more than a little bit excited over all of these possibilities.

"For all three, they're teen romances, so all are a familiar genre, but one of the movies is dystopian. Which, of course, you have the last say, but I would rule that out."

"I'm not against ruling it out, but do you mind explaining why you think I should?" I ask, wanting to hear her opinion. I'm pretty sure it has to do with the fact that all of the world sees me as a dainty and romantic girl, not a gun-wielding and government-overthrowing girl. Which, I can change in the future, but not just yet at the beginning of my career.

"To start, they always take much longer to film, due to

all of the special effects, which could really slow down your career, but also because it will ruin the whimsical, romantic, and cute vibe you have going. One of the top reviews we get about you is that you feel like the cute girl next door. I think that changing that right now would be quite a risky move." Marie finishes.

"Okay, I think I agree with you on this one, and that for now, we should just say it's not a priority." I agree, understanding where she's coming from.

"Sounds good. And, remember that we're not making any final decisions today. We're going to have your parents and lawyer go over all of this before I send the final word to anyone."

"Yes, of course," I reply, giving her a nod.

"Perfect. The next movie is a travel romance, so lots of different locations. If I can remember properly without going through my files, the main characters are enemies, but their parents are friends, and they're going on a European trip for the summer." She takes a breath and glances at her desk. "Yes, that is correct. Right now, travel is all of the rage, and so are enemies to lovers. That one has a lot of potential, so that should definitely be on your radar."

"I really like the sound of that one, actually. Would there be a lot of actual traveling?" I question, the idea of filming a movie *and* getting to travel causing excitement to bubble within me.

"Definitely. They want this movie as authentic as possible, so most of it will be shot in Europe. Only a few of the stunts—don't worry, there aren't very many—will be done in LA in a studio." Marie replies, glancing at her last stack of papers. "And for the last one, it's a western television series that follows a family as the children grow up and fall in love. To me, the premise is beautiful and so cute, but it *is* a series."

"Which means?" I ask, not knowing what she's getting at. My phone chimes and vibrates in my purse, and I have to resist the urge to check it.

"This means the filming for it will be much longer, and it's slated for a few seasons, to follow each girl. So while you would be the star of one season, the other ones will just have you as a background character. It might be worth it to skip for now, because you'll be wasting so much precious time to only be seen for a few minutes per episode." Marie explains, her reasoning sounding solid.

"And I wouldn't be able to work on other projects as this one is being filmed?" The idea of a series is kind of exciting, but I do understand what she's saying about not wanting to waste my time on a series that won't benefit me much past my season.

"If the filming isn't too intense, then I'm sure that could be worked into your contract. The thing is, this series and the travel movie are set to begin filming in mid-December. So even if you wanted to do both, it's not really possible for you to be in Europe and Montana—that's where the western one will be filmed—at the same time." Marie says with an apologetic look.

Her words are beginning to sound like she has a bias towards the travel movie, but I can see where her thought process is coming from, and why she thinks it will be best for my career. "Oh. Well, that's kind of sad. I was really liking the idea of a series, and then other movies on the side."

"I completely agree. And maybe you'll have a change of

heart and decide to do whichever you prefer. This is just my professional advice, since I've been in this industry for a very long time. The final decision is yours." Marie says gently, reminding me that I have full control over my career.

"Okay. I'm going to think about it all, but I'm pretty sure it will have to be the travel movie." I say, shifting my eyes to the paper that's marked *Summer's Mirage.* "When is Summer's Mirage being released?"

"This isn't a definite date, yet, but they're thinking October twenty-sixth, with the premiere being the day before," Marie says, her eyes skimming the paper. "And the press interviews being on the twenty-sixth and seventh, maybe longer depending on the want for more interviews."

"Wow, that's a while. I haven't been too interested in what's going on in the movie world, since we just moved, and I'm busy with some other things."

"That's totally understandable." Marie agrees, looking into my eyes before speaking again. "If I were you, and this is just me personally, I would be very careful about how much you pay attention to the movie and celebrity world. On and off social media. While this is a fun job, being in the public spotlight can be both dangerous and tiring. Which brings me to our next topic."

"And that is?" Although I know what she's going to say, I allow her to bring it up herself.

"Kai." Yep. Here we have it. The root of a lot of my problems right now. "He's still telling you that he's going to tell the media that you were unprofessional on set?" Marie questions.

"Yeah, he is. However, last night I met a guy who offered to be in a few social media photos, that way it would throw

Kai off." While Santiago didn't exactly offer himself up, he did agree, so it's not *too* far from the truth.

"Really?" Marie asks, gears turning in her head as she mulls this over. "Honestly, that's kind of a great idea. As long as he stays anonymous, then once this has blown over, you can go on like nothing happened."

"That's what I was thinking. That way Kai will have just about nothing to use against me because I can say that we were dating the whole time." I say, explaining my thought process.

"I think this will actually work. We just need Kai to stop being so salty over the fact that you were never interested in him, so he stops this nonsense about you being unprofessional on set." Marie huffs, clearly exasperated with this whole situation. Technically, he hasn't done anything yet, but in recent interviews, he's very subtly hinted at the fact that I tried to date him, which is far from the truth. He was the one who was always making unwanted advances on me—none of which went far—and when I rejected him, he became upset and is now trying to spin a story in which I'm the anti-hero. The problem is that he hasn't actually done anything that we can take legal action with.

"Thank you. I think this should work, too. It will be much harder to spin a story like that when I'm in a relationship. He'll look crazy for trying to sell a story about me trying to date him after I've already posted another guy on social media." I say, trying to convince myself this will work. Besides the fact that I don't want my professional reputation to be slandered over him having feelings for me and spinning a story that it was the other way around, I'd also like to not be barely a year into my carer and opening a legal battle against my co-star. Not a very good look.

"It's not a problem, Brooklynn. I see a lot of talent and a long future in this business, and I don't want your career muddied before it's even really started." I can see the honesty in her face, and although I'm weary of most people claiming to care about me, my parents and I all agree that Marie really does have my best career intentions at heart.

"Thank you for looking out for me. I don't think I would be here without you." I say this as we exchange a quick hug, our meeting adjourned for now. Just as I'm exiting the door, Marie answers. "You would be just as far with or without me. Your talent is yours alone. No one but you owns it, and it's my job to make sure that it stays that way." I smile back at her, the door closing softly as I walk down the hallway.

My phone chimes again, and I'm reminded of the earlier message that came through while I was with Marie. Opening my phone, I see that there's finally a response from Santiago, but the message that came while I was in my meeting, is from Kai.

CHAPTER 5

Santiago

"Carmen, it's time to go." I call into Carmen's room, the warning Mother gave me before she left replaying through my mind. Her words had been serious and strict. Don't be late with Carmen. I know that she's just stressed about being looked down upon by everyone at the club, but she should remember that she's an Alvarez. The whole club is in the palm of her and Father's hand.

Later, once we're in the car and en route to The Enchanted Ivy, I pull out my phone and check the messages that have accumulated this afternoon. A few are from my friends, but the one that I notice and pay attention to is Brooklynn's. She messaged me earlier, and I'd replied, asking her if her family has an Enchanted Ivy membership. She responded a bit later, saying that they didn't, but her father is going to inquire about one, since they're new to the area. I don't bother mentioning that there's no price tag on one, since the owners have more than enough money of their own. They just enjoy the exclusivity of having their own club and inviting who they like. If I were a betting man, I would say that they'll easily allow the Carmine family in, but only time will tell.

I message back an acknowledgment of her message, then slide my phone into my pocket. This evening is going to drag out, and my best bet at surviving the night without becoming overly annoyed is to find a quiet corner or room to hang out in. I know that with the nature of tonight's silly party, there will be nothing interesting for me to do.

"Santiago?" I turn as we enter the main room, Mother taking Carmen's arm, and Matteo turning to me.

"Yes?"

"Don't..." He trails off for a moment before speaking again. "Don't do anything to ruin Carmen's night. She's still making a first impression, and most everyone here is a little bit weary after they've watched you these last few years." Matteo finishes.

My jaw tightens at his insinuation, but I try to play my words off as a joke. "Don't worry, Matteo. Besides, everyone knows that you're the perfect son, not me." I say, giving him a fake salute.

"Santiago, don't. Not right now." Matteo hisses, as if he doesn't know that I'm the outcast among our family. He's the perfect son who graduated college early, I'm the rebellious son who can never seem to get his act under control, and Carmen is the perfect daughter. The youngest in the family, and brand new to this crazy life of ours.

To say that she's been sheltered is an understatement. My parents have never brought her into the business or party world—until now—and what comes with that is her not knowing much about my past. That's not to say it's terrible or even extremely mentionable, but I'm known as the wild child, and as of now, Carmen is to never know about any of it. She's the only one in my family who doesn't look down upon me for my not-so-great decisions of the past.

School is tiring as always, even more so with the party last night. I'm not sure why I'm expected to attend every party, even the ones that land on school nights. It's not that I'm necessarily tired, just tired of people. I rolled into bed at around three this morning, only to have a fitful night of sleep that left me drained when I woke up at seven. The only thing I have to be grateful for is that Blackstone Academy has later classes, allowing me to sleep just a little bit longer than I normally would if I were to be attending school somewhere else.

As I settle into my desk, an all too familiar figure takes a seat next to me at his desk.

Alessandro Valentino.

Assigned seating really needs to be outlawed. I know that if it were up to him, he would be sitting as far as possible from me, but of course our school must have this control over us.

The name makes me feel sick and angry all at once, and I have to remind myself that I know how to act civilly around him. I did it all of last year, and the year before that. It's not as impossible as it feels right now.

He clears his throat, and it takes all of my willpower to not glance over. Why must he be so noisy in class? Has he ever heard of respecting the teacher? I almost scoff at my thoughts, since I don't mind other students doing whatever they please during class.

Being on my ex-friends list really leaves you a short list of things that you can do that don't annoy me. And pretty much his breathing is enough to irritate me.

Later, after we arrive home, there's a message from Brooklynn on my phone, asking if I'd like to meet at a local restaurant for dinner. I reply with a yes, and slide behind the wheel of my car to meet her. I'm not too sure why she wants to meet me, but a chance to not have to go over every detail regarding my day at school is a chance I'll take.

CHAPTER 6

Brooklynn

Santiago said he'd be here, but here I am, still waiting for him. After another ten minutes, I'm just about to leave, but his figure is just now appearing through the restaurant's glass doors.

"Brooklynn, I'm sorry for being late. Something happened on the way here, and I needed to take a quick detour." Santiago says coolly, before speaking to the hostess and arranging for her to take us to our table. It's under my name since I had the idea to come here, but he just takes charge and walks one step behind me on the way to our table.

"It's fine," I say, taking a breath before speaking again. "Although I was just about to leave because I was sure you were going to spend your evening elsewhere."

"I wouldn't dream of it. Even if I were to not come, I would have told you." Santiago assures me, sounding shocked at the idea of him leaving me.

I don't have the chance to respond before we arrive at

our table in the secluded area of the restaurant. While it's not like I've been followed here by paparazzi, I still glance around the room as a precautionary measure, just in case. The price of a meal here is enough to deter the average person, and the security that was near the front door was enough to convince me that this should be okay.

My social media following has been steadily growing by the day, and my publicist informed me today that the paparazzi have been on the lookout for me since they haven't caught wind of my family moving.

"So, how did you spend your day?" I ask Santiago after we place our orders for dinner.

"At school. What about you? Shouldn't you still be in school, seeing as you're seventeen?" Santiago responds, looking at me curiously.

"Technically, yes. However, since I just moved, my credits haven't transferred yet. I think I start on the tenth." I say, trying to remember which day Dad said it would be. "But, you'll be seeing me before then, because Mom said we were approved for a membership for The Enchanted Ivy. Are there any upcoming parties, by the way? I just got the most adorable dress, and I *need* to wear it somewhere."

Santiago chuckles, a small smile working its way up his face before responding. "I think there's an upcoming garden party. Will your dress work for that?" His mention of it going with the event sends a weird feeling throughout my body, because no boy has ever asked me.

"It should work perfectly, actually. It's white with small pink bows and flowers on it, and it's probably just about knee-length. Would that work with the party theme?" I ask, contemplating for a moment before speaking again.

"Actually, don't answer that. I'm going to wear it regardless of whether it will fit with the dress code." I say with a wave of my hand. Santiago smiles at this, and I give him a quizzical glance, unsure of what I've missed. "What's so funny?"

"Nothing at all. I was just thinking." Santiago replies smoothly, checking his watch before speaking again. "So, what did you have planned for tonight?"

Planned for tonight? My mind scrambles to find the meaning of his words, and then I'm reminded of my original plan. "Oh, that, I just need to take a few photos of you—not your face or anything—so that I can post them. If Kai takes any longer to acknowledge you, I might actually lose my mind." I take a sip of my soda before speaking again. "He actually messaged me today, if you can believe it. He wanted to congratulate me on my splash into the acting world, and how well I'm being received. He very conveniently left out the part about seeing you on my social media, which was *so* annoying." I huff, crossing my arms.

"So he's your co-star as well as the reason you need a fake boyfriend?" Is Santiago's only takeaway from my whole monologue.

"Who told you?" I ask, trying to figure out where he got that knowledge. I certainly haven't said that, right? I've been careful to not mention anything about who all of this fake boyfriend stuff is about.

"You just said, 'If Kai takes any longer to acknowledge you, I might actually lose my mind'," Santiago says easily, as if he just said the sky is blue.

"What? Are you sure I said that?" I question, staring deep into his light brown eyes, the color of them mirroring dark apple cider. A color I haven't even thought to associate with eyes until now.

"Positive." Santiago says, not even pausing before responding.

"Well, I guess you might have heard me correctly," I say, careful to not say that he's right, because I'm not going to give him the satisfaction of knowing I just slipped up. "But this is strictly confidential information. We're just trying to get Kai to realize that creating fake accusations against me is even more pointless." I say with a shrug.

"So what is he trying to say about you?" Santiago asks curiously.

"That I tried to date him on set, and that I was unprofessional," I answer with a roll of my eyes.

"And that's not true, right? How does you 'dating' me change the outcome of this?"

"Well, he hasn't exactly gone to the press or social media with all of this, so if he sees that I'm in a relationship, and there's already proof of that on social media," I gesture to Santiago before continuing, "then there are two outcomes. One being he just drops it all, since he'll realize that his claims sound more baseless. And two being that if he does go somewhere with the story, everyone will assume he's making it up out of jealousy." I explain.

"That's actually a good idea. I just have a question though. Why is he making all of this up?" Santiago questions, his eyebrows furrowed.

"Because *he* tried to date *me* and I rejected him. Now he's bitter, especially since my career is taking off much faster than his did. This is a last-ditch effort to ruin me before my career has even fully started."

"Oh, I see. So why don't you go to the press with that story?" Santiago asks, as though this is the most obvious answer.

"My publicist. She claims that it will ruin my image if I go around exposing the world's biggest heartthrob right out of the gate."

"Why?"

"All of his fans will go rabid—which will happen if he continues with this—and 'I could ruin his career by speaking poorly about him'." I quote, rolling my eyes. "I wouldn't be intentionally trying to ruin him, but my publicist seems to think that all teenage girls are out to get their exes. Which, isn't even fair, since he's not my ex."

"That's more than a little unfair. Especially since he's doing this to you. Well, not exactly, but trying to." Santiago says, his eyebrows raised at the audacity of this situation.

"Well, at this moment, if he tries to move much further than just telling me he's going to say all of this, then we're going to take legal action. The problem is we don't want it to get to that point, because *that* is a story for the press." I explain, Santiago nodding along now that he fully understands the story.

We don't have any more time to talk, because just then, our food is delivered. The waitress sets our plates, giving me a sidelong glance before turning to walk away, and my stomach clenches at the thought of her spreading gossip about me being out with Santiago Alvarez. Fine, I'll admit that I *did* know who he was before we met, but only because I'd seen a headline about him a few months ago. It was something about his parents buying him shares in a large company, and how he and his siblings are set to all be billionaires by twenty-five. So what if I was slightly dishonest about knowing him before? My excuse for it is that I honestly didn't remember it was him until after talking to him for a while. When his friend said that he would be coming, the name didn't even register in my mind until way later.

Santiago clears his throat before speaking, and I raise my eyes to watch him. "So when are you going to photograph me? I feel like I look pretty good right now." I press my hands to my face, trying to stifle laughter. I feel a blush heating on my cheeks as I imagine people watching us. Instead of responding to him, I pull out my phone and snap a few photos of our plates, his plate across the table, and one with his torso in it, but no neck or face, that way no one will be able to use some technology to analyze his skin tone and match it to him or something. You never know these days.

"There. Now you may go back to your previously not good-looking self." I tease, poking fun at how he said he looks good right now.

"But I thought you said I look good?" Santiago asks, feigning confusion.

"Now when did I say that?" I say, trying to remember a time tonight that I said anything go the sort.

"When you first met me. Don't you remember?"

"How would I remember saying that?" I ask, the memory coming back now. "And do you just memorize everything I say? Maybe you need to take my job since you're so good at memorizing lines." I exclaim.

"I remember most conversations. It's a quirk of mine, I guess. Some people have a photographic memory, and I have... whatever memorizing dialogue is." Santiago says with a chuckle, reaching over to pick up his cup and raise it to his lips. I watch him curiously, trying to understand what exactly he means by that.

"So you could just tell me what conversations you were having on..." I trail off, trying to find an obscure date. "Right now two years ago." I watch as his face shifts into an uncomfortable expression for a split second before straightening into his usual relaxed face.

"I was talking to my friend about our plans for the evening." He says vaguely, almost like he's trying to work around the question. To most, it would sound normal, but as an actress, I have a pretty good detector when it comes to someone shifting into a masked version of themselves.

"What did you end up doing that night?" I question, more than a little bit interested in his answer.

"We went to The Enchanted Ivy." He says calmly, giving me a relaxed look, as if he's awaiting my next question. And I almost ask him about what conversations they had, but I can tell that if I were to ask, he wouldn't say. Instead, I move in a more positive direction.

"So you really do know your stuff. I'll keep that in mind for later." I say with a smile, taking a bite of my food and giving him a playful wink.

"I'll be looking forward to it."

CHAPTER 7

Brooklynn

When our waitress brings the check, I reach into my purse, pulling out my wallet, only to hear Santiago telling her that he's going to be paying for the whole meal. What?

"Oh, I'll be paying for my own food. Don't worry." I rush out, waving my hand in a nonchalant gesture.

"Don't listen to her. Here, take this, please." Santiago says, passing the waitress his card, completely disregarding my protests.

"Okay, then. I'll be back in one moment." The waitress says, taking his card and walking to the front of the restaurant, not even fazed by our disagreement.

"Santiago, really? If anything, I should be paying for your meal, since you were invited." I say, dropping my wallet back into my purse. This man really is impossible.

"Nonsense." Santiago responds, taking a sip of his drink.

"Nonsense? What do you mean?"

"I mean, it's nonsense that you think you have to pay for your food, much less, mine." Santiago answers simply.

That's something I find exceedingly interesting about him. Everything is cool and collected as if he's had hours to practice his lines before speaking them.

"You're difficult to figure out." I eventually say, giving him a sidelong glance as I brush a few curls out of my face.

"Good." Santiago says smugly, taking his card from the waitress as she drops it off.

"*Good*?"

"Yes, good. Not knowing your opponent's head is the most infuriating and unsettling thing, you know?"

"And I'm your opponent?" I question, Santiago's direction of the conversation completely confusing me.

"No, of course not. But if you were to figure me out, who's to say that someone else wouldn't be able to?" Santiago says easily.

"Who is your opponent if it's—thankfully—not me?" I question, leaning closer to him, the table between us. The longer we talk, the more the sounds of the restaurant fade, creating this sense of false loneliness.

"Everyone. If I'm to succeed in the business world, then I must keep everything to myself." Santiago takes a breath before speaking again, as if considering something. "Why are so happy that you're not my opponent?"

I raise an eyebrow before responding. "Why would I *want* to be your enemy? I'm literally using you right now. The last thing I need is you being a second Kai in my life." Pressing my lips together, I realize how my last few words sound. I realize how harsh my words sound, but they're the truth. I don't need someone else intentionally against me.

Santiago's eyes soften for a moment as if he's realizing the accidental vulnerability in my words. "Unlike some people, I'm rather committed to someone once they need something of me."

"Well, that's good to know. What do people usually need of you? I'd hate to be your second fake girlfriend." I say teasingly, trying to lighten the mood after dragging it down.

"The title of fake girlfriend is yours, and yours alone. I can confidently say that you're the first and last one I'll ever have." Santiago says with a smirk.

"Did I ruin your experience with fake girlfriends?" I ask, wondering if he means this in a good way or a bad way. Not that fake girlfriends are normal, but still.

"Not at all. I just don't think it would look great on my dating record to have multiple fake girlfriends."

"You have a dating record?" I choke out, the sound of it more than a little bit silly.

"Well, yeah. Doesn't everyone?"

"I mean, I guess so. Does that mean that you have a long dating history?" I question. "Let me guess, you're a playboy who has a million girls in line to date him, and I'm currently ruining your chances of ever getting a girlfriend."

"My dating history isn't exactly *long*, but I don't like committing to a relationship that will only be a short one." Santiago answers, giving me a quizzical glance before speaking again. "And why would you ruin my chances of having a girlfriend?"

"Because I'm obviously the best—albeit fake—girlfriend you'll ever have," I say with my award-winning smile, giving Santiago a wink. Santiago doesn't say anything to this. Instead, he leans back in his seat and smirks.

Saturday arrives quickly, and with that, comes the garden party that Santiago informed me of. My parents are more than excited to make new friends, and with that, comes their excitement to leave early.

"Mom, I'll be out in a few minutes!" I call out of my bathroom door, her voice coming from my bedroom door. I'm finishing the final touches on my makeup, and need just a few more minutes before I can call it perfect. My dress is already on, and my shoes are by the door, so this really is the last thing I need to do before leaving.

Adding the last layer of mascara and glitter eyeshadow, I smile as the lip products I use are still applied to perfection. Slipping on my heels, I grab my purse—I had to change from my usual purse because the colors didn't match just right—and close my bedroom door behind me, rushing outside to find my parents in the back seat of one of their limousines.

"You look so adorable, honey." Mother exclaims with a smile, reaching out to push a few curls from my face as she does so.

"Thank you, Mom," I say, buckling my seatbelt and brushing my hands down my skirt as I turn to face the window.

After arriving at The Enchanted Ivy, I'm greeted with the soft sound of a classical band playing and the chatter of people. A much different atmosphere than the party I met Santiago at. Mom and Dad approach a few of the groups of people, introducing themselves. A smile rises on my face as I watch people quickly recognize them, welcoming them with open arms.

Around me, the sights and sounds are almost overwhelmingly beautiful, but peaceful at the same time. The music and humming of chatter are familiar, but the small droplets of water that land near my feet—a product of the small water fountain—mixed with the fluttering of butterflies and chirps of birds is enough to leave me slightly dazed. The low, evening light that flows through the gardens around me basks us in golden light, and it creates an aura of warmth and comfort. Leaning down to brush my fingertips across the petals of a soft pink flower, a throat clears behind me.

"I think you're the first person here to give those flowers a second glance." Santiago's deep voice says from directly behind me.

"Oh, well, was I not supposed to?" I gasp, his voice startling me.

"Of course not. I was merely mentioning that no one else has given them a second thought." Santiago replies, raising his hands in a no-offense gesture. "But do you have a guilty conscience, Brooklynn? Why so defensive?" Santiago teases, raising an eyebrow. I straighten, squaring my shoulders.

"No, not at all. I just thought it was an odd thing for you to say." I retort, cocking a hip as I wait for his response. I'm not sure why I'm giving him such a hard time, but I can't make myself stop.

"What an odd thing of me to say. I apologize." Santiago says, throwing me a smirk my way before shifting his body to face the garden pathways. "Do you want to take a walk?" My head tilts slightly as the change in topic switches.

"Sure, Santiago," I say, falling into step next to Santiago as he walks along one of the paths. "I like your name, by the way." The words tumble out of my mouth, and I feel a slight bit of embarrassment at my sudden proclamation. "I mean, of course I like it. Who wouldn't? I just thought that you might like to know that I think it's pretty."

"Noted. I think Santiago is a nice name, but I've had a few people tell me that it's a strange one." Santiago says with a slight smile. "Also, I do like knowing what you're thinking about me. It makes you a little bit less mysterious." He admits, running his fingers through his hair before dropping it back by his side.

"Me? Mysterious?" I gasp, stumbling slightly. Santiago quickly reaches out to stabilize my elbow, as if it's second nature to him. "What on earth makes me mysterious? I'm quite literally the definition of an open book. In fact, if you were to open the dictionary, my name and photo would be right next to it."

"I don't think so at all. You're *so* confusing." Santiago says with a laugh, his tuxedo sleeve brushing my arm as he does so.

"How am I confusing?" I demand, indignant.

"You met me, and within five minutes you were trying to ask me about people there, then you were telling me that you wanted me to pose as your boyfriend, then you invited me to dinner where you picked my brain for two hours, then you're out here, doing...this." Santiago finishes, looking me up and down as he speaks.

"I guess to the intellectually challenged, then my motives

might be hard to understand, but I'll break it down for you." I tease, knocking my shoulder against his arm before I continue. I'm grateful for the quick friendship that Santiago and I have formed because this would be quite a difficult operation if we weren't friendly with each other. "I was told to talk to you by one of your- friends, and when I saw you, I thought you would be the perfect man for the job. Then I saw that guy—whatever his name was—and thought he was cute, then you said you didn't like him, so I went back to my original plan of using you. Which you agreed to pretty quickly-"

"I didn't have much of a chance to decline." Santiago interrupts. I don't even stop talking, rather I just talk over him and continue.

"And then after that, I thought to myself, 'why don't I invite him to dinner since I know nothing about this guy who is my fake boyfriend. I didn't even have the intention to pick your brain, but you're a rather interesting man, Santiago. I couldn't help myself from asking you things that I've been wondering." I say with a smile as if it should be obvious.

"Thank you for explaining to the intellectually challenged. Now, I'd like one more answer," Santiago says, smirking before continuing. "Why is Kai so salty you rejected him? And why do I get the feeling you took it upon yourself to create this whole ruse?"

"That's two questions, dear," I say, patting his arm. "And you're not getting an answer to either. Ask me something easier, and then maybe."

"So I have to tell you everything, and I'm entitled to nothing from you?" Santiago asks, half incredulously.

"Precisely. Let's remember, you *did* agree to this." I say with a half-apologetic shrug, as if he should have prepared for this when he said yes to fake dating me.

"Where exactly was this disclosed in our contract? And where exactly is this contract? I feel like you're adding rules to it by the minute." Santiago teases, a chuckle escaping him.

"It's in my head, but since this is your first time fake dating somebody, I'll let you in on the basic rules. Number one, don't ask questions. Number two, play along like your life depends on it. Number three, don't fall in love." I say simply. "That last one shouldn't be too hard for you since you know that I'm not dating anyone for the time being, but that first one, you might struggle with."

"Very clear and concise. May I ask where these rules came from? I'm a little bit hurt that you've had other fake boyfriends before." Santiago says playfully.

"Oh, you're my first, but definitely the last." I truthfully respond. "As for the rules, they're universal rules, Santiago. Every fake relationship goes off of those rules. Have you no romantic culturing in your life?" I tease, the question a genuine one.

"I'm sure that Carmen has shown me a romantic book or movie before, but I'm not a fan of the fictional world."

"*Carmen?*" I exclaim, wondering just who this Carmen girl is.

"Yeah?"

"Who is she?" I demand, protective over *my* fake boyfriend.

"Jealous much?" Santiago teases, glancing down at me before continuing. "She's my younger sister. She's your age, actually. Maybe a few months younger."

Santiago has a sister? "Of course I'm not jealous. I was just surprised, that's all. How come you never told me that you have a sister? Let me guess, you have a brother, too?" I say, exasperatedly.

"I do have an older brother, but that's it. I'm the middle child." Santiago answers. "What about you? Do you have siblings?"

"Of course not. I would have mentioned that pretty early on, don't you think?"

"So, what, you just thought that I was an only child?" Santiago questions, genuinely curious.

"Um, yeah. I kind of thought that somewhere in our conversation you would mention them if they existed." I take a pause. "So can Carmen and I become friends? I feel weird asking, but I think that it would be weird to just go up to her and say something like, 'Hey, I'm using your brother, but do you want to be friends?' don't you think?"

"No. I don't want anyone in my family finding out about this, yet." Santiago answers quickly.

"So now I'm your dirty secret!" I exclaim, not really caring, since I'm hiding his identity from the world.

"Whatever. But I was yours, first." Santiago teases back, the chatter of the party sounding louder and louder as we round a turn, and I realize that we've made a full loop around the garden.

"Yeah, yeah. Whatever you need to say to feel better about yourself." I say, laughter escaping me.

"I think this is where our evening will be ending. Acting like we're already close probably isn't the best look for your plan." Santiago says before slipping away towards a group of men.

"Hello, Brooklynn. Your parents told me that you'd be hanging around here, and I've been wanting to introduce myself." A woman says approaching me, her golden skin shining in the dusk light.

"Hello, miss..." I trail off as I have no idea who this woman is.

"Oh, sorry about that. I'm Mrs. Valentino. I always forget that there are people here who don't know who I am." She says, as though my not knowing her name is the most laughable thing in the world. I fight the urge to raise an eyebrow at her, but I restrain myself.

"How lovely to meet you. Did you have anything you wanted to speak to me about?" I ask, reminding her that she's the one who approached me.

"I just wanted to introduce myself and show you to anything you might need." Mrs. Valentino answers, as if just now realizing how strange she must seem to me.

"It was lovely meeting you. I'll be sure to find you if I need anything. You seem to know a lot about this place." I say with a smile, giving her ego a boost. If I'm going to reject her invitation, then I might as well not make her hate me.

"All right then. Have a lovely evening Brooklynn." Mrs. Valentino finally says, understanding that I'm letting her down easy.

"You as well," I respond, her figure disappearing in the crowds of people that are surrounding me. What a strange interaction.

As the evening fades into night, I find myself desperate to leave. It's not that I dislike it here or something bad has happened, but I'm just tired and bored. Maybe it's a sign of immaturity, but I would rather be at home, in my cozy bed, rather than talk to people all evening, not recognizing a single face other than Santiago's.

Santiago, who, I can't talk to, per his request. While I don't know exactly what he meant about him not having a great reputation or whatever, I see the old ladies who have nothing better to do besides gossip give him sidelong glances every now and then.

"I love your outfit! May I ask where it's from?" A female voice questions, her voice alerting me to her approaching figure. She looks to be around twenty-one, and I can't quite place where I've seen her, but she looks familiar.

"Thank you. I'm actually not sure where it's from, my mom bought it as a gift, but thank you." I respond, the woman unfazed by my response.

"No problem. Are you with anyone tonight?" She asks, chewing on her lower lip as she asks this.

"I'm not, why?"

"This is my first time being back here, so I kind of need to look like I have friends before some elderly lady asks me to marry her grandson or something." She says, not even sounding the slightest bit like she's joking. "Oh, I'm Daniela, by the way."

"Well, it's nice to meet you, Daniela. I'm Brooklynn, but you probably already knew that." I extend my hand for a handshake, but Daniela pulls me into a quick hug.

"Thank you for this. I know I probably sound so weird right now, but I just needed to escape the older people of the party for a bit. I'm sure you understand, to an extent." Daniela says with an exasperated sigh. We talk for a moment before my eyes instinctively move to Santiago, and I realize that Daniela's eyes move right along with mine.

"Santiago Alvarez?" Daniela asks with a raised eyebrow, her gaze moving back to look me up and down before they land back on Santiago.

"What do you mean?" I ask, feigning confusion at her words. She obviously doesn't know that we're fake dating, but from her tone alone, she knows that something is up.

"You picked a bad boy as the first guy to crush on here?"

"Well, I never confirmed that we even know each other, but even if we do, what do you mean by bad boy?" I question, needing to maintain the small amount of secrecy that I have.

"Santiago is just...a bad boy. He's maybe not the textbook definition, but he's always been in fights—some physical, some not—finding cracks in the rules, things like that." Daniela says with a shrug. "He's not a bad guy or anything, but he's rougher around the edges. Well, as rough as a boy who wears tuxedos more than casual wear can be. Santiago has always been a little bit different than his family and has always wanted to be seen as more than just the middle child. The younger brother, you know?"

"You said that you used to come here, but it sounds like you know more about this place than I originally thought," I comment, anticipating her reaction.

"Yeah, I guess so. I grew up here." She takes a breath. "I went to school at Blackstone Academy, spent my nights at parties here, and the first chance that I got, I left, and promised to never come back," Daniela admits, her voice taking on a new tone that I can't quite decipher.

"Why-"

"Brooklynn, I think we're going to be leaving now. It's already much later than we planned to be out, and the roads at night might not be the safest." Mom says, she and Dad nearing me.

"Okay, I'm coming." I turn to Daniela, an understanding expression on her face. "I'm so sorry, but I have to leave."

"Go right ahead, Brooklynn. I had a lovely time talking to you, and I hope that things work out for you." Daniela says, giving me a small wave before making her way into the groups of people mingling in small circles.

CHAPTER 8

Brooklynn

The ringing of my phone awakens me, and it must be the sleep-induced delirium coursing through my veins, because I answer it without even checking the caller identification.

"Hello?" I answer groggily.

"Brooklynn?" A deep voice I'd recognize anywhere says through the line. Sitting up so quickly that my head spins, I right myself before speaking again.

"Kai?" The words come out as a question, but there's no way it's someone else.

"The one and only." He says with a chuckle. "How are you doing, Brooklynn?" I consider just hanging up, but the thought of being able to slip Santiago—not his name—into the conversation stops me from doing so.

"I haven't been too bad. How about you?" This is the safest thing to say, but it still leaves a bitter taste in my mouth.

"Same old. All of the acting gigs are taking over my life,

but it's fun. How are you settling into your new place?" Kai asks.

"Being here is an adjustment, but not necessarily a bad one. I'm meeting people, learning my way around a new mansion, you know." I answer truthfully, unsure of what else to say.

"About meeting new people..." Kai's voice trails, and now I know why he's calling. The photos of Santiago. "Have you met anyone in particular?"

"What do you mean?"

"Nothing." He says quickly. Too quickly.

"Why did you call?" I finally ask, annoyance slipping into my tone.

"No reason. I just wanted to hear your voice, I guess." Kai answers coolly, as though calling someone at four in the morning is a common occurrence. Biting my lip, debating on whether I should press for an answer, but deciding against it, I tell him that I need to hang up, and without giving him a chance to respond, I click the button to end our call.

"You're Brooklynn Carmine, right?" A boy asks as I fumble with my locker combination, the lock unfamiliar to me. Smiling so as not to seem rude, I nod.

"Yeah, that's me. What's your name?" I respond, extending my free hand for a handshake.

"I'm Hardin, nice to meet you." He says as if considering

something before speaking again. "I didn't realize you were attending school here."

"Today is my first day, so don't feel bad." Smiling as I say this, I try my locker combination again, finally opening it. "However, if you happen to come across someone talking about me, please let them know that I would love it if they kept my attendance on the down low." I finish, deciding that this boy is trustworthy enough.

"Sure, I can do that. Why would I, though? Everyone here knows that it's school policy not to discuss the students with any outside parties. Sorry to tell you, but you're not the first celebrity to attend here."

Wow. Dad did a nice job finding the perfect school for me. Now his reasoning that I wouldn't need a bodyguard during school makes sense. "Thank you for letting me know. And don't feel sorry or anything. I'm not offended." Placing a few books in my locker, I turn back to the boy—Hardin—and smile. "It was nice meeting you."

His disappointment is visible, but it's better to let him know that I'm not interested in him. "Nice to meet you, too. I'll see you around then?" I nod, but I'm pretty sure the only times we'll be seeing each other are on the rare occasion we pass in the hallway.

"Who was that?" A familiar voice asks from behind me as Hardin walks away, my body now turned to face my locker as I finish with my books.

"Shouldn't you know? I'm the new student here." I say with a smile, turning to face Santiago as he takes a few steps closer.

"Yeah, but I don't usually have sixteen-year-old boys

introducing themselves to me while I add books to my locker." Santiago argues back, an easy smile on his face.

"I guess so," I reply, closing my locker and leaning against it as I pull out a piece of pink gum from my bag.

"So who was he?" Santiago questions again, as though he actually cares.

"Why?" I press, innocently looking up into Santiago's eyes as I wait for his response. The dark color is actually rather beautiful, and with the right roles, he could very easily become the next teen heartthrob. The way that his eyes are set so perfectly to his face, matched with the depth behind them, is dangerous. A flash of jealousy slips through me at the thought of millions of girls pining after him, and I blink my eyes a few times to center myself back to reality.

"Earth to Brooklynn." Santiago says jokingly, waving a hand in front of my eyes, and it's then that I realize he responded to me and is now trying to get my attention.

"Oh, what?" Blinking a few times, I glance up, hoping that my staring wasn't too obvious.

"I said that I was merely curious, and then you never responded." Santiago replies, eyeing me suspiciously as though he'll be able to decipher my strange behavior by just meeting my eyes.

"Sorry. I was just thinking about that party." Is the first thing that comes to mind.

"Did you have fun?" Santiago questions, giving me a quizzical glance before turning to peer down the hall as someone he must know watches us. I can't see the look Santiago gives him, but I can see the reaction, and that's enough to let me know that he understands. What he understands, I'm unsure of.

"Yeah, I really did. After being with you, I met someone named Daniela. She was really nice, and we talked for a while." I answer, more sure of myself now. I watch Santiago for a reaction to my words, since my suspicions about him and Daniela knowing each other are still there.

"That's nice. What's your first class?" Santiago responds, changing the topic. Interesting. Peering at my schedule, I find the correct hour and read Santiago the name. "You'll be over in this direction, then. I think you'll share some classes with Carmen, by the way." He says, gesturing in the direction of a long hallway.

"And I'm not allowed to talk to her," I say glumly, giving Santiago a quick glare, the feat difficult with tons of students walking around us.

"Oh my gosh, you're acting like I'm a controlling and manipulative husband or something. I just don't want her—or anyone—to get the wrong idea and to start spreading rumors." Santiago says exasperatedly, mock rolling his eyes.

"And Carmen would do that?" I ask with a raised eyebrow. "What if she saw us right now? What would she say?"

"She wouldn't, but she also wouldn't understand why we're doing this. If she saw us right now, she would probably assume that I'm showing you to your classroom, and nothing more." Santiago answers.

"Why wouldn't she understand?" I press, Santiago's reasoning strange. She's my age. Why wouldn't she understand?

"She just wouldn't. No one in my family would." Santiago's words are firm, and I drop the subject. Apparently, this is a touchy topic.

"Sorry," I say, the words coming out even softer than I'd intended. Whatever Santiago has against his family, knowing about our little fake dating arrangement isn't something that we're going to be discussing in the school hallways.

CHAPTER 9

Santiago

Brooklynn really knows how to find the cracks in my exterior, and every time she easily finds one, without seemingly looking, it reminds me that I need to keep to myself. I never agreed to Brooklynn prying into my personal life when I agreed to be her fake boyfriend.

I don't even think that half of the time she's intentionally doing it, and that scares me even more. How can someone so easily find all of my weakest points and know just what questions to ask?

These questions swirl in my mind for days, leaving me unable to sleep, the worry and unrest making me even more irritable than I usually am.

CHAPTER 10

Brooklynn

The rest of September flies by with school and the occasional party, but for the most part, it's relaxing.

When I rise from bed, I check my calendar for the day, noting that there's a party at The Enchanted Ivy, and I make a mental note to be ready early. Santiago will be there, and while I'm not too *worried,* it's been a little bit since I've seen and conversed with him.

By five, I'm completely ready to leave, although our driver won't be ready to pick us up until six.

My outfit consists of a pink midi dress and pink heels to match it. It's maybe not the most extravagant outfit I've created, but it's definitely still beautiful.

Arriving at the party, I feel eyes on me as I enter the room, and I have to remind myself that this is just because we're still new here. And Xander Carmine is quite famous. More famous than most people here.

"Brooklynn, you look nice." Santiago says as he nears me, his figure coming from across the room as I enter.

"Thank you, Santiago. You clean up..." I look him up and down, as if I really need to find something to say before finishing my sentence. "Nicely."

Santiago's lips curve in a smile, and my eyes subconsciously trail to his eyes as I wait for his response to my joke. "I've been told that on occasion. In fact, another woman told me something like that fifteen minutes ago." He says with a wink.

"What? Where is she?" I move my eyes across the room as I try to find this mystery woman. Why is she telling Santiago that? Does she really mean that? Or is she close enough to him that she also teases him?

"Ah, the jealousy that Brooklynn tries so hard to conceal is back." Santiago says, wrapping his arm around my shoulder as we walk down one of the many hallways. I shiver from his touch for a second, but before he can remove his arm, I lean into Santiago's shoulder.

"*Jealousy?*" I exclaim, pouting my lower lip as I look up into Santiago's beautiful eyes.

"That's what it sounded like." Santiago says through a chuckle. "However, I'm not sure how you can be jealous of someone's other relationships when you avoid them for nearly a month."

"Hey, not fair. I've been...busy." I answer quickly, Santiago's words letting on to the fact that it's not just glaringly obvious to me, but also to him.

"Busy avoiding me." Santiago says, as though I should just stop trying to defend myself. He's right, though. And I was doing a good job of it until tonight. His tone isn't mean; rather, it's like he's just stating the obvious.

"Well, I wasn't exactly avoiding *you*. It was more than

that." I respond, trying to find the reason I've been so absent recently.

"I get it. You just moved here, you're starting a new school, and you have a new movie coming out in a month, right?" Santiago questions, his voice genuinely happy for me.

"So you've been keeping up with the tabloids then?" I tease, as though no one is talking about Summer's Mirage. Quite the opposite, actually. Every time I open my phone, there's a notification or article about how I'm going to be in it, alongside Kai. I'm not sure that the movie's media team is letting on that Summer's Mirage was filmed last summer, well before Our Story, but I've kept my mouth shut about it.

"What? Of course not." Santiago exclaims, as though I've accused him of tripping an old lady or stealing a child's candy.

"With that reaction…" Something about seeing Santiago squirm, when he so obviously usually has control, is the most amusing thing in the world.

"You're literally so impossible, Brooklynn. I can't even have a conversation with you." Santiago says exasperatedly, sighing as though I'm placing the weight of the world on his shoulders.

"So were you reading the tabloids?" I finally ask a few minutes later as we near the party. While I'm curious about what he has to say, I almost hope that he says no.

"Not really. I just saw something about it on social media. When were you going to tell me about it, though?" Santiago questions, as if I were supposed to tell him everything about my life.

"I don't know." The answer is blunt, but truthful.

"With all that's been going on, I kind of thought that you already knew."

"Friends are supposed to tell friends things." Santiago teases, but I can tell that he's not hurt. "Especially friends who are fake-dating. How lousy of a boyfriend would I be if I didn't know when your movie is releasing?"

"Oh my gosh, I get it," I say with an exasperated huff. "I'm sorry for wounding you, dear Santiago."

"I'm just joking. It would be easy to figure out." Santiago says easily.

"No, you're right. Even if you were just joking, friends *do* tell each other things. You're literally posing as my boyfriend, and I can't be bothered to tell you what my schedule looks like. That kind of makes me a bad friend."

"No, it doesn't." Santiago scoffs. "There are many worse things you could do that would make you a bad friend."

"Like?"

"I don't know. I'm just sure there could be worse things." Santiago answers quickly. *Too quickly.*

"So you have ex-friends, then? Good to know." I whisper before breaking away from him and walking straight into the middle of the sea of people, curious as to whether he'll follow me.

On rare occasions, I feel as though I know nothing about Santiago. Like he's just a boy I walked up to and chose out of a crowd—even though that's kind of what happened—and not someone I know. But as I shift my head slightly, Santiago's body is only a few feet behind me as he follows. Except, instead of wrapping his arm around my shoulder like before, he stays those few feet behind me.

An hour or so later, the party is still in full swing. "Hey, I'm going to go grab another soda. Do you want one?" I ask Santiago as I stand.

"I can go grab those, don't worry." Santiago replies, briskly standing and reaching for the drink.

"That wasn't my question, Santiago," I say in a singsong voice, fully intending on getting my own drink, and going to the restroom. There's no way I'm just going to say that out loud, though. Santiago really needs to learn how to take a hint.

"Are you-"

"Absolutely." And with that, I spin and make my way through the clusters of people around the room. Passing a waitress my empty drink, I use the restrooms, and just after reaching the main room, a voice shouts out something unintelligible, and gasps of horror ricochet around the room.

"What's..." The words are a whisper on my lips as I try to find the source of the commotion, except there's no way for me to even move towards the middle of the room, because everyone in the entire world is crowded around whatever is happening.

"Someone get them both out of here! What a menace to our beautiful party." A woman exclaims, sounding angry and shocked.

"I agree! Why are we allowing these two children to ruin our event? How dare they." A man's voice shouts, his tone even angrier than the woman's before him.

What is going on?

"For everyone's information, I'm twenty years old. I'm not a mere child who can be scolded when I was clearly the victim in this situation." A voice that is completely unfamiliar to me says dangerously calmly, as though he's been waiting for this moment.

"Oh, and I'm just-" *Santiago?* Oh my gosh, whatever is happening, Santiago is involved. There's a venom in his tone that I've never heard before, and I desperately wish that people would move out of my way so I can view the problem.

"I think Mr. Alvarez needs to leave the party. I'm not sure exactly what happened, but I do know that I heard his voice first, and we *all* know what a hot temper he has." A woman who sounds vaguely familiar says, as though she has full control of the situation, and she's the appointed judge.

Words around me are spoken, but the whole room suddenly feels very stuffy, and the urge to vomit rises in my body. Scrambling back to the bathroom, ten minutes pass before I'm able to emerge again, and by then, everyone is continuing with their party as though nothing has happened.

Spotting a younger waiter, I approach him quickly before he can leave. "Excuse me, what happened with those two men?" The desperation in my voice must sound strange, but he just raises his eyebrows as if questioning where I've been.

"There was a scuffle between two of the party attendees, and one of them was asked to leave." He says, his tone neutral, and I'm sure it's because he probably shouldn't be giving me his version of the story.

"Thank you so much, sir." I'm turning when his hand quickly reaches out and grasps my arm before quickly dropping it.

"Hey, I'm not supposed to be gossiping or whatever, so please don't mention that I'm the one who told you that." His voice is slightly concerned, and I can understand where he's coming from. This is his job, and he's sacrificing it just to give me the answers that I'm desperate for.

"Don't worry. I don't even know your name, nor do I remember speaking to you." I say with a smile and a wink, bringing a smile to the waiter's face.

"Thank you." He says, turning to get back to work.

"Thank *you*."

With my heels clicking on the polished floors, I dart towards the door with the intention of finding Santiago before he leaves, curiosity and worry filling my insides. This is unlike Santiago, right? Throwing open the door and rushing into the cool night air, there's not a trace of Santiago anywhere.

A tear slips down my cheek as images of a hurt Santiago flood my mind, and I sink to the steps. Obviously, something happened, and it was bad. Bad enough that he had to leave. If I had been here, or if I had let him go get the drinks, would this have happened?

"Brooklynn?" A gentle voice calls into the night, the large doors closing softly. Wiping my tears—careful not to smudge my makeup—I stand.

"Yes?"

"It's me, Daniela. I saw you leave and was worried about you." She says, closing the door and moving to stand next to me. "What just happened was a lot, and I know that there's...something between you and Santiago."

"I never-" I begin, immediately cut off by Daniela.

"Don't even. I saw the way you reacted when you heard him. Whatever it was, I know that you care for him. And, I do too. In a weird, older sister way that I can't quite explain." Daniela begins. "But you also have to know that he's always been a hothead and reckless."

"I don't care about that. I just want him to be okay." I finally say, a tear running down my cheek.

"He will be, Brooklynn. You just..." Daniela sucks in a deep breath as if searching for the right words. "You need to protect yourself and your peace. Santiago isn't going to magically change, and being reckless is just about as natural to him as breathing is."

"What are you saying?" I whisper, Daniela's words becoming jumbled in my mind. "What are you telling me to do?" Even if I don't listen to whatever Daniela is about to say, for some reason, I want to know her insight into Santiago. She must know a lot more about him and his family than she's letting on, her point-blank summary of him telling.

"I'm not telling you to do something. Rather, I just want you to be careful with your emotions. This is your life, Brooklynn. I can't tell you to do anything, nor should I." Daniela says truthfully, giving me a smile before retreating back to the party.

What am I supposed to do with this information? Calling Mom, I let her know that I'm going to have our driver take me home early, and once he arrives, I climb into the backseat. My head rests against the window as soft music plays over the car speakers, and just as I'm finally feeling calmed, a text comes through on my phone, the contact information reading that it's from Santiago.

CHAPTER 11

Santiago

Every inch of my body feels hot and angry, and just sitting next to Matteo and Carmen makes it so much worse. It shouldn't, seeing as they're my siblings, but being around anyone—including them—is difficult right now. Emilio's words echo throughout my mind, and the desperate wish to have hit him immediately is strong. Why did I hesitate in shock and allow him a chance to evade the punishment he deserved? Blocking the disgusting things he said, I press my head on the window, the cool air actually doing some good for my pounding head. The level of disgust that's boiling in my body is surely causing it, but I would rather walk home than say anything. Carmen has already tried twice to ask about what happened, but between my anger and Matteo's urge to keep everything under control, she doesn't know. To be honest, I'm not sure if even Matteo knows what really happened.

The idea of Emilio saying something even somewhat similar about Carmen brings a wave of nausea throughout my body, and I have to remove my mind from the last part of my evening. Deciding on something a little bit safer, my thoughts drift to Brooklynn.

I remember Brooklynn saying something about the tabloids and how I shouldn't read them, but the curiosity nags at me—if not this, then I'll go back to my previous thoughts—and I give in to searching her name on my browser. What could she be so worried about me finding? She seemed genuinely serious about not looking her up.

After a few minutes, it becomes *very* apparent why she didn't want me to search her up. Besides finding a few hate articles, her photo appears next to the photo of an older man that all of the United States could recognize.

Xander Carmine is Brooklynn's father.

Why didn't I ever put two and two together and realize that Brooklynn is the daughter of the most famous actor of my parents' generation? I've seen hundreds of movies and television shows with him in them. Xander Carmine is practically the most well-known actor in the world. Maybe the least well-known thing about him is that he has a daughter. To be fair, I didn't know that he's Brooklynn's father, but then again, I don't do anything other than watch the movies he's in.

Scrolling a moment longer, my eyes catch on a headline that suddenly makes me feel guilty for recognizing her father a few minutes ago.

BROOKLYNN CARMINE'S OVERNIGHT SUCCESS ISN'T BECAUSE OF HER 'PHENOMENAL ACTING', RATHER IT'S BECAUSE OF HER FATHER, WORLD FAMOUS ACTOR, XANDER CARMINE.

I tap on the article, and it's full of disgusting and hateful words, the writing of an angry teenager. Clearly, it's from a well-known journalist, but the contents feel as though a jealous friend would have written something this rude.

"Brooklynn's success story is one of a fairytale. A new actress being paired with the world's largest teen heartthrob in a romantic movie that follows the story of them gently falling in love. Cute, isn't it? That is, until you realize how much of her success has been handed to her. With a father as well-known as Xander, it wouldn't be too hard to pull a few strings to land such a major role, right?"

I close the app before finishing the article, the anger within me bubbling to the surface again. How dare someone write such a nasty review? And about Brooklynn, of all people! She's more than deserving of the roles she's played. Her acting is amazing, and she's an amazing person in general. Sure, I've never seen her act, but I'm sure it's phenomenal.

Not being able to imagine that anyone could dislike her, I toss my phone aside, running my hand through my hair. I'm not sure if she's seen this, but I never want her to.

So now, on top of a night where I was put to shame for the filth of Emilio, thoughts of people hating Brooklynn are also going to be heavy on my mind. Just great.

My resolve only lasts for a few minutes before I pick up my phone again, my fingers tapping out a quick message to Brooklynn. Her response is instant, and a small smile forms on my face as I imagine her seeing my message and responding to it before doing anything else.

Just as soon as this thought appears, I force it away. Why in the world would I be imagining Brooklynn responding to me before anyone else? And why is that making me giddy?

CHAPTER 12

Brooklynn

Per Santiago's cryptic request after countless messages for him to tell me what happened, I'm meeting him for a drive. The party last night left my sleep restless, and when he finally relented to telling me what happened, he said that it needed to be in person. Naturally, I told him that I'd meet him as soon as possible, which also happens to be eleven at night.

It's not my fault that I was busy in meetings all afternoon with my publicist. She's not too happy about all of the backlash that has been rising these past few weeks as more and more people realize that my dad is Xander Carmine. There's no more time to think about the problems of my public life—as far as I'm concerned, I couldn't be happier that my dad is Xander Carmine—because Santiago is pulling up at the entrance gates to my house. Slipping through the side gate, I move to the passenger door, which Santiago has already opened. The first thing that hits me is the scent of his car. It's not bad; rather, it's the opposite. The smell is—whatever it is—intoxicating.

"Hi, Brooklynn." Santiago says coolly, closing the door behind me as I buckle my belt. He swiftly rounds his car and slides behind the steering wheel, guiding his car onto the road. I snap a quick photo for my social media as his hand rests on the steering wheel, the blurry city lights out the window.

With my anticipation for an answer as to what happened last night, words start tumbling from my mouth. "So, now that you're trapped in this car with me, you're going to give me exactly what I want," I say, turning in my seat to face him. My skirt twists with me, and I smooth it down as I speak. "You have to-"

"One might hear you and think that I'm stuck in a dangerous situation. With you demanding that I do exactly as you say, while I'm trapped in a vehicle with you." Santiago interrupts, glancing over for a split second, an amused smile on his face.

"*Santiago!*" I half yelp, half hiss. "I can't believe you would say such a thing. Seriously, you're so childish. I want you to tell me what happened last night at the party. I don't want anything else from you."

"Says the girl who just took a photo of me to use in her elaborate plan." Santiago quips back, a sly smile replacing his previously amused one. He did *not* just say that. Laughter escapes him, and I fight off a smile. I love how we can be like this. How we can argue, but not really be arguing.

"How dare you. You agreed to being used, now stop bringing it up in *every* conversation." I say with an exasperated sigh. "Just tell me what happened, will you? It's not nice to keep things like this from friends." And for some reason, I can't help myself from the next words that spill from my mouth. "Especially not from fake girlfriends."

"You've got me there. I guess I can't keep things from my fake girlfriend, even though I was going to keep it from my *friend*." He emphasizes the 'friend' part, but I don't dwell on it.

"Yes, I do. Now, tell me, *what happened?*"

The humor that previously occupied Santiago's face fades, and he chews his puffy lip for a moment before speaking. "That is kind of a loaded question, but I'll try to go over it as best as I can." Santiago sucks in a breath, tapping his fingers on the wheel. "There was this guy, Emilio, and all evening I'd been getting a weird feeling from him. I brushed it off, though. He just...every time I saw him, there was this weird sense of anger that I felt towards him."

"And?" I question, needing him to elaborate more.

"He just made me angry whenever I looked at him. I couldn't figure out why, but it went on all night." He glances out his mirror as a car passes us, taking a pause. "And then when you left to go get your drink—which took a while, by the way—he said something so disgusting that I was stunned for a minute, and-"

"What did he say?" I exclaim, annoyed at Santiago for just completely leaving the most important part of the story.

"Well, I'm not going to be repeating it right now. That's not what's important. What's important is that even *I* was clutching my pearls in horror. Then-"

"Santiago, are you *really* not going to tell me what he said? I can't believe you." I huff, frustration rising in my body.

"I'm not going to repeat it, Brooklynn. Really, I'm not going to." Santiago says firmly. More firmly than he's ever spoken to me. Well, he can play at this for a while, but I'll figure it out sooner or later. I'll let him have this for right now, but Santiago hasn't seen me when I want something.

"Whatever. Keep going with your story." I say with an eye roll.

"After the shock of what he said wore off—which was maybe two seconds—I swung at him, with the full intention of hitting him square in the face." A gasp escapes me at the thought of Santiago *hitting* someone. Seriously, that's not Santiago. "But since I was stunned for that moment, he had the chance to move. And then that's when everyone else got involved, and you pretty much know the rest." Santiago concludes, glancing over to gauge my reaction to his story.

"What a story." I lament, not knowing what else to say. What else is there to say?

"Quite the story you were expecting, right?" Santiago says with a chuckle, but there's no humor in it.

"Something like that." Taking a pause, I debate my next words, unsure of how else to phrase them. "Would you mind taking me back home?" It's not that I want to leave, but tomorrow there's school, and these last few days have left me drained. I also know that if I stay in here any longer with Santiago, we'll keep talking and end up not going home for another few hours.

Santiago appears confused by the question but nods his head. Did he have plans for us besides talking? "Yeah, of course. I can get on the right road if I use that parking lot. There's road work on this next road." Santiago explains, flicking on his blinker as he turns into the abandoned parking lot.

"If someone were listening to *you*, they would be concerned for me, with this little abandoned parking lot and all." I tease, echoing his earlier joke.

"Yeah, yeah, Brooklynn. Let's remember who the driver is." Santiago teases back. As his car turns, his lights land on a car parked directly in the middle of the lot. "What in the world?" He questions as the car in front of us immediately starts speeding off.

"That's...strange. Why are they leaving?" I question, my eyes following the car as we pull up close behind it, waiting to turn onto the road.

"Better question is why he's here." Santiago says cryptically.

"He? How are you sure it's not a girl?"

"Well, I guess I don't *know*, but I'm assuming it's a guy." Santiago sputters, caught off-guard by my question. "But maybe there is a girl in there or something."

"See, Santiago, I expect better of you. Just assuming that there's a guy in there and acting like you're certain is misleading for people. Not me, of course, but people would just believe you without questioning you." Clicking my tongue as I speak, it seems to only go in one ear and out the other with the amount of attention he's paying me. "Hello? Earth to Santiago."

"Still here, just driving. If you've forgotten, I'll enlighten you to the fact that this is actually pretty dangerous, and that I need to keep most of my attention here."

"Or you're just reeling from the fact that you're wrong."

"Or I'm trying to keep us alive." Santiago retorts back.

"Or-" I squint my eyes for a moment, the darkness making it hard for me to see. "Hey, isn't that the car from earlier? The one from the parking lot?" I ask as we drive down the highway.

"In front of us? Yes. I guess we're going in the same direction as them." Santiago muses, his tone sounding as though he finds it amusing. The car is driving considerably faster than us, but it seems to still be within the speed limit. It's another few minutes before Santiago speaks again, and when he does, it sounds as though he's been considering his words carefully. "So, regarding your ex, Kai, is he reacting the way you hoped he would to all of the photos?" Santiago questions, sounding more than interested in my answer. Which, I guess, is normal since he's a key piece in this operation.

"Well, I mean, kind of?" I finally say, unsure of how to explain the cryptic messages Kai has been sending me all month. He's tried to start conversations with me, and while I've kept it civil, he's acting less and less like he's a loose cannon.

"Kind of?" Santiago presses.

"Yes, kind of. It's complicated, but I promise that all of our photos are being put to good use." I offer, not sure how else I can dodge the questions. It's not that I don't want to tell him, it's just that it's hard to fully explain how Kai acts. His personality is totally strange, and I don't feel like unloading all of his cryptic messages.

"Complicated? Aren't we past that?" Santiago teases, considering his next words before speaking. "Haven't we been past that since you asked me to be your fake boyfriend?"

"Santiago"

"Just kidding. You really shouldn't have let on how much you dislike me bringing that up." Santiago says, not a hint of remorse in his words.

"Goodness, you're quite shameless, aren't you?" I tease, knowing that he *is* quite shameless, even without the Kai factor.

"Of course. There has to be at least one Alvarez with a shameless personality." He replies, his words sounding deeper than just his simple sentence.

"What's that even supposed to mean?" The words tumble from my mouth, and I don't even know why I'm saying them. Why do I want to know the deeper meaning behind his words? Santiago is just...a friend.

"Whatever you'd like it to mean." Santiago says simply, as if he's telling me his favorite ice cream flavor.

"Santiago Alvarez, you're literally the most annoying person in the world." I huff, crossing my arms in somewhat mock frustration.

"Brooklynn Carmine, you're literally the most confusing person in the world." Santiago responds immediately, not missing a beat.

We drive in silence for the last few minutes of the ride home, and as Santiago stops in front of my house, I almost wish that we could do over the whole drive again, if only to spend more time together.

"Good night, Brooklynn." Santiago says as I step out of the car, a smile on his face as he closes the door behind me. I turn to face him before walking through the gate, and give him a smile of my own.

"Good night, Santiago. Have a safe drive home." I say,

patting his arm before retreating to the front door. I'm not sure why, but just before stepping through the doorway, my body twists in hopes of spotting Santiago's car driving off. Instead of glancing at his taillights, I'm glancing into Santiago's eyes, his body still in the same position it was when he opened the car door for me.

His smile is one that sears a burn in my mind, and in this moment, for whatever reason, I'll never forget the expression that his face wears. It's one that I've never seen in real life or in the movies. It's maybe the most...*pure* expression I've witnessed in my entire life.

CHAPTER 13

Santiago

It's stupid, really. Stupid for a whole bunch of reasons, but mostly because I don't know why it's happening.

Why can't I control the smile that has carved itself into my face, and why can't I shake it?

Something about Brooklynn has caused this silly smile to permanently reside on my face, and I'm not sure if I like it, or if it concerns me.

Thursday arrives with the promise of a lively party at The Enchanted Ivy, and as I dress in one of my tuxedos, thoughts of Brooklynn consume me. I'm not entirely sure why, but thoughts of seeing her, spending time together, and just being around her are exciting. Really, it's ridiculous, but try telling my brain that.

Once outside and in the garage, I meet Matteo, who seems to have had the same idea as I.

"Do you want to drive your car in? I'm thinking about taking mine." Matteo asks, leaning against his car.

"Yeah, I'm going to." I reply, briskly feeling self-conscious under his gaze, Matteo's face saying something that he won't speak out loud.

After sorting out who Carmen will ride with—we can't just let her ride alone—she slides into my passenger seat. Once her buckle is latched, I move my car through the front gates and onto the road.

In true Carmen fashion, she asks too many questions—not that they frustrate me, but they get tiring after a while—and soon enough we're at The Enchanted Ivy. I drop Carmen off near the front entrance and drive my car to the nearby parking area.

Yes, I could just allow one of the staff here to park my car, but one of the many things I've learned during these busy parties is to never pass your keys off. I would much rather take an extra five minutes of my life to safely park my car, instead of learn that the valet drivers were busy with so many cars that mine got bumped or scratched.

"Santiago, wait for me!" Brooklynn exclaims, climbing out of the backseat of what appears to be her family's car, their driver continuing to drive once she's out. Her parents walk towards the door, leaving her out here with me, their conversation about needing to give their driver a raise.

"Good evening to you, too, Brooklynn." I tease, her abrupt entrance endearing.

"Goodness, now you're acting like I jumped you or something. I was just excited." Brooklynn huffs, her short strides working hard to keep up with my pace. Subtly slowing, we fall into step next to each other as we enter The Enchanted Ivy.

"Well, that's pretty close to what happened." The words slide easily from my lips as I watch her expression twist into one of fake annoyance.

"Whatever, then. I guess you won't learn why I'm excited." Brooklynn says slyly, giving me a wink before turning away from me.

"Wait, I'm sorry. Please tell me what you're excited about." I plead, only half faking my desperation.

"Fine, then. Your begging is *so* embarrassing, though." Brooklynn concludes, the smirk on her face devious. And now, I come to the conclusion that she would have told me anyway. That's just the kind of girl she is. Always excited about something, always ready to talk.

"Go ahead, I'm listening." I encourage, walking with her to one of the sofas that line the walls.

"Whoa, now. Don't you think that sitting together is a little bit incriminating? What if someone sees us?" Brooklynn says, hesitating as she sits.

"What's so scandalous about us sitting together?" I question, genuinely confused.

"Well, I guess nothing to do with our arrangement, but you know how...*older* people are." She says, her words saying that she's trying to find a nicer word than *old* to use for the people in attendance here.

"Yeah, I do. Besides a few fan rumors, we should be fine." I say this as I eye the older crowd in front of us, their gossip audible from twenty feet away.

"Fans?" Brooklynn questions, confusion obvious on her

face. "What do you mean? I thought that there was no paparazzi here?"

"There isn't. I just meant all of the old ladies who saw us together at the party."

"So they were watching us? That's...comforting." Brooklynn says, sounding not the least bit comforted. I can understand where she's coming from, but with the people here, you just have to take whatever they say and let it go in one ear and out the other. The older generation that frequents here are people who spent their lives in front of a camera or behind a desk at their billion-dollar business. They have nothing else to do besides gossip. It does fuel a lot of my anger whenever it becomes overwhelming, but recently, I've been trying to find peace with the fact that I can't control whatever they say, and that I need to just let it roll off my shoulder.

"Not really. Like you just said, *older* people tend to be quite the gossips." I tease, knowing that she'll crack a smile at this. To my prediction, she does smile at this, and just seeing it brings a smile to my face.

"I guess so," Brooklynn says, scooting closer so that her shoulder is pressed against mine. I'm surprised at the contact, but not uncomfortable. Everything with Brooklynn is both confusing and calming at the same time.

I'm happy with our friendship—albeit a strange one— and it's moments like this when I remember that she's just about the only person to see this side of me. Without meaning to, most people see my hothead side. The side that doesn't have rational thinking or polite people skills.

Brooklynn seems to naturally bring out my funny, calm side, and for the life of me, I can't figure out why.

"So, are you going to tell me why you ambushed me outside?" I say slyly, turning to watch her expression change into one that looks like she's about to start laughing.

"Okay, I'll admit that I was pretty excited, but *ambush* is a strong word. I'll let you off this time, but don't push your luck anymore." Brooklynn says, patting my arm. "What I've been trying to tell you for the last twenty minutes is that I have another movie coming up. I'm going to be the *star* in a travel romantic comedy. It's a young adult, of course, and the location for filing will be all over Europe." She gushes, her eyes wide and excited.

"Wow. That's...amazing, Brooklynn. I'm really happy for you. When will you start filming?" My excitement for her is dampened by the thought of her not being here all of the time, which is crazy, because it's not like her filming movies in the United States would be much different. I guess the thought of her not always being here hasn't crossed my mind.

"I know, right? They wanted me specifically, and I only had to do one little tape just to make sure I'm the right fit. Obviously, I am, since they made the final decision and all." Brooklynn continues, her brown eyes getting more and more excited the longer she speaks.

"Of course, they wanted you. They would be crazy not to want you." I respond truthfully.

"You think so?" Brooklynn asks, her eyebrows raised. "I mean, I know that I'm a pretty good actress, but them just reaching out to me before announcing anything about it was pretty crazy."

"Absolutely. I know so."

"Santiago!" An all too familiar voice calls out, the words

causing irritation to rise within me. "Get over here, man. We've been waiting for you." Lyle's voice carries from about twenty feet away, and I have to resist the urge to roll my eyes in public.

"Hey, isn't that one of your friends?" Brooklynn whispers, moving her eyes to Lyle's annoying figure.

"Not really. We're in the same friend groups, and he's pretty annoying." I whisper back, matching her lowered voice.

"So are you going to go over there?" She whispers, this time closer to my ear. Brooklynn's breath grazes my neck, and for whatever reason, goosebumps flood my neck and shoulders.

"Maybe. Do you want me to stay?" My words come out even lower than before, my face even closer to her. It's a strange feeling when she abruptly pulls away from me, but not as strange as the face she's making.

"It's not up to me," Brooklynn responds, her tone a normal one, now. "And why are you whispering?"

CHAPTER 14

Brooklynn

Santiago's expression is one of confusion, his light, golden skin wondering as he sucks in a breath. I almost wonder if he's going to say anything, but eventually he speaks again.

"I'll see you in a little bit. As annoying as Lyle is, I should probably go see him and the rest of his minions before they turn on me." Santiago says this as he stands, and I almost grab his arm and drag him back down, so that he'll explain the reasoning behind his words.

Of course, I don't. Instead, I watch as he moves through the crowds of people towards the group of men—all around the same age as Santiago—and stands near them as they talk and laugh. His demeanor is completely different than when he was with me, and for some reason, this piques my interest.

Is this his normal demeanor? I guess I've never seen him in a public setting other than at school or these parties, but during those times, he's either right with me, or nowhere to be found.

Either way, it's physically impossible to keep my eyes off of him as he mingles with his friends, and for a moment, I'm envious of him. Besides Santiago, I don't have any friends here. Maybe it's because I'm new here, or maybe it's because I haven't really tried. Santiago has been enough for me.

"You're *what*?" I question as I fully comprehend his words.

"You heard me. I'm dating Rachel. I have been for the past few weeks." Kai's voice comes through the line clear and crisp, no emotion in his words, as though he's telling me of the weather that's predicted for tomorrow.

"And you thought to just tell me now?" Relief floods through me at the thought of him dropping his false accusations against me. Well, I'm hoping this is what his new relationship will lead to.

"Why not? We're friends, right? You're dating someone, right?" Kai asks through the phone speaker. So he did notice all of the Santiago photos I've been posting. I wonder if this is his way of verifying that I'm with someone, rather than him telling me that he's dating someone.

"Yeah, I guess so. I'm happy for you." I reply, staring absently at the wall as he says goodbye and hangs up the phone. He's nothing more than a co-star to me, contrary to his idea that we're friends.

Co-star.

Oh my gosh. Kai will be at the premiere and press interviews for Summer's Mirage. What if this is all an act, and he plans on going crazy at the premiere?

It's been ten days since the auction, when Santiago abruptly left me to hang out with his friends, and then went home early with his sister, but tomorrow there's a dinner party at the club, and that will be the perfect time for me to find Santiago and tell him that our Kai problem is—mostly—behind us. That also means there's no reason for us to continue fake dating, which also means we're not going to see each other nearly as often. Maybe I'll plead for him to still be my friend—who am I kidding, I'm *not* doing that—and we'll still meet and hang out sometimes, because over these past few weeks Santiago has really become a friend to me. It seems strange to even think about *not* being friends with him.

It feels like a weight has been lifted from my chest, now that Kai is out of the picture. As if his presence was not only mentally weighing me down, but physically, too.

CHAPTER 15

Brooklynn

Sunlight streams through my open windows, and it's a full five minutes of basking in God's glorious sunrise before I remember that it's Monday. Frantically checking my phone's clock, I find that it's well past when my first class would have started. Well, there goes my near-perfect attendance.

At least when Dad enrolled me, he made sure to tell the principal that I would probably miss in-person classes, but to send my lessons for those days to my email, and they would be finished by the allotted time. Having Xander Carmine for a father—as well as just being an actress—is a real perk to life.

Pulling up social media on my phone, I'm horrified to spot photo after photo, video after video, and article after article detailing Kai's twisted story of how things went on set for Summer's Mirage and Our Story.

How in the world did anyone get wind of this? Replaying my conversation with Kai last night, it dawns on me that he did this. He was unhappy that Santiago and I are "dating". After skimming a few articles, they pretty much all say the same thing: I fell in love on set for Summer's Mirage, then he rejected me, and I was insufferable throughout the filming of Our Story. Which is a complete lie, and sends fury through my blood.

"Santiago, I need you," I whisper, grabbing his arm as he moves past me. "Come on." Pulling him to one of the hallways in The Enchanted Ivy, I stop once we're not visible to someone just passing by the entrance to the hallway.

"What's up?" Santiago asks, confusion and concern in his voice.

"Don't act like you haven't seen Kai try to rip down my career, brick by brick," I say, only a hint of humor in my tone.

"Oh, that." Santiago says with a wince, as though realizing how touchy this topic is. "So I gather this plan didn't work?"

"You're absolutely correct. And, you're going to help me." I say simply, as though it's already been decided.

"And how will I do that?" Santiago doesn't sound displeased, but he definitely sounds stressed. Impulsively, I reach out and place one hand on his cheek, studying his eyes. His cheek is warm and soft under my touch, and the contact from his skin sets mine on fire.

"Are you okay?" The words tumble from my mouth, and it's a reminder that I'm only one person in this operation. Santiago is the other half to this, and I can't just demand things of him, no matter how much I'd like to.

Santiago stiffens at my words, but doesn't say anything for a moment. "Kind of. I'm not in danger or anything, but I'm going through some stuff right now." Santiago answers truthfully, sounding fully honest in his words. "I've been processing some stuff, but I don't mind helping you. In fact, I think it might be good for me."

"Are you sure? I'm sorry for just assuming that-"

"You're fine, Brooklynn. Tell me, what do you need?" Santiago says, sounding fully like he means it.

"I kind of need you to-"

"Santiago, come, join us for a quick game of golf." A man calls out from down the hallway. Glancing up, it's suddenly obvious that my hand is still resting on Santiago's face, and I drop it immediately. Who is this man who thinks he gets to just waltz in and demand that Santiago go wherever he pleases? That's *my* privilege, not his.

"Go, Santiago. Let's meet later tonight after the party is over." I say quickly, not wanting anyone to hear my plan, other than Santiago.

"Are you sure? I can just tell him that I'll play another day."

"Positive. Text me later when you're outside my house." I whisper, turning from him and walking in the opposite direction from the man who wants to play golf with Santiago. This will work better, anyway. There wouldn't have been enough time to go over everything the way I'd like if we were trying to do it in a hallway, during a party.

The text from Santiago chimes on my phone at one in the morning, and for the briefest of seconds, I consider not answering it.

No. That would make me a horrible person, because yet again, I'm dragging Santiago down another one of—my well-executed—plans. I would be the jerk of the century if I ignored him.

Responding and letting him know that I'll be outside in a few minutes, I run my hand down the black leggings I'm wearing, and consider my pink, oversized sweater. It should be warm enough since it's not that cold outside. Picking up my purse—you never know what you may need—and phone, I slide on sandals and rush out of the house, towards the gate. One of the security guards gives me a quizzical glance as I leave the property, but I know from past experience that he doesn't care where I'm going, so long as it's consensual. It's not his job to parent or police me, just to make sure that there are no trespassers or paparazzi outside our home.

Santiago is waiting outside the passenger door, opening it as soon as I approach. "Thank you so much for coming this late," I say with a smile, sliding into the seat as he closes the door.

"So, tell me what's urgent enough that we need to be meeting at one in the morning." Santiago says with a chuckle, his hands resting in his lap.

"Well, first, let's remember that I did try to talk to you at the party, but one of your friends needed you," I reply indignantly, half joking. "And why aren't you driving?"

"Neither of those things has anything to do with you needing me, by the way." Is Santiago's only response, and have to roll my eyes at the level of sass on this man. "But to answer you, it's because you never said you wanted to go anywhere, and wouldn't it be breaking the law to just drive away with you?"

"Goodness, Santiago. I didn't realize you were such a rule-follower. Just drive somewhere, because it's a little strange to have the security team watching us as we just sit here and talk." Santiago's expression changes into one of confusion, and maybe...hurt? I'm not sure what I said to cause this, but before I can ask, his expression is back to the humorous one it was before.

"I can drive wherever I'd like?" Santiago questions deviously, glancing over before sliding his car into drive. What in the world must he mean by this?

"Well, as long as it's not somewhere crazy-"

"Don't worry, Brooklynn. I don't plan on taking you anywhere far." Santiago reassures me, as if realizing how worrisome his words might have been. "I'm not going to tell you where we're going, though. That part is confidential."

"Confidential? I don't like the sound of that." I say with a light giggle.

"Absolutely. You can't be the one who keeps all of the secrets, right?" Santiago teases pointedly, obviously getting at the fact that I still haven't told him what I need him for. I can't believe how many times we try to have a conversation, but then end up talking about everything else. Everything with Santiago is just so easy. Something

I'm realizing is that this almost never happens with anyone else.

"I see where you're going with that, you know?" I tease, giving him a pointed look.

"Then tell me what you need me to do." His words stir something within me, and it's his willingness to just do whatever I need him to do, even if he hasn't heard my plan yet.

"So, you—as well as every single other person on earth—have seen the ten trillion articles detailing that Kai told the press, and how it paints me in a bad light, right?" I start, the words sounding too cheery for how much this could really affect my career.

"Well, I wouldn't say that-"

"That's all I need to hear. My dad said that the lawyers are already taking action against him, but there's still another problem." Taking a breath, I glance over to gauge his reaction. "My master plan includes you accompanying me to the Summer's Mirage premiere as my boyfriend."

"Oh, well, isn't that maybe the opposite of what you should do? Shouldn't you show up alone since by then all of this should be taken down?"

"Santiago, I really wish life were that simple, but sadly, it's not. You being there is the only way to fully remove attention from those stories, while legal action is taken. Not to inflate your ego or anything, but you're not bad looking, and that will get the press talking."

"Well, I'm glad I'm not too good-looking or anything." Santiago chuckles, my choice of words amusing to him.

"Goodness, you're better looking than Kai, and the rest of the actors our age. Are you happy now?"

"Much. Continue with this master plan of yours."

"So then, you'll be the perfect boyfriend, and the press will stop having a field day with Kai's story, and they'll just be reporting about my mystery man as our lawyers get all of the other stories taken down."

"How-"

"Hush, please, I'm still speaking. We're never going to mention you by name, nor will we have actual photos together; rather, you'll be on the sidelines until we enter and leave, and you'll be a few steps behind me the whole time."

"And has your publicist agreed to this? I feel like this might...leave you in more hot water than you're already in." Santiago says gently, not exactly opposed to the idea, but cautious.

"Of course. We created the plan together—not that I mentioned your name or anything—and my manager also agreed to it. They're not so much worried about the whole dating thing, but they *are* worried about how this little scandal will look to future casting directors, because Kai made up that this was on set. Which is a big no-no in the acting world."

"Why?" Santiago is genuinely curious, and I smile at his want to know more about my world.

"For starters, if the actors start dating, then they'll usually try to add in more scenes of them together, and they become easily distracted on set. That's two of the reasons, at least."

"And the others?"

"Well, if they break up, then it's the opposite of that one. All of the romantic parts aren't really romantic, because usually, the actors aren't on the best of terms. Other than that, if their relationship is public, then if they break up before or during the release, that's all the press will be reporting on."

"Which is bad, because movie press is everything? Not the actors' dating lives?" Santiago questions.

"Exactly. Most of the outcomes—good or bad—damage the movie's publicity, and that's *never* a good thing." The words that my dad told me over and over play through my mind as I remember him telling me that I needed to be careful with Kai. At the time, it seemed silly to think that he would like me, and even sillier to think that he would make something like this up. Now, here I am, dealing with the aftermath of not listening to the weight of Dad's words.

"Well, this is quite the predicament, but I'm in." Santiago says easily, as if being invited to be eaten by the wolves is an everyday thing. "Besides, it's not like my life isn't being shaken up, already."

"What do you mean?" This is his second mention of something being wrong in his life, and I don't exactly like spilling all of my problems to him, only for him to hold his close.

"It's noth-"

"Don't even, Santiago. We're in this too deep to be hiding stuff like this from each other."

"Wow, you really must want to know." Santiago teases, his humor masking the vulnerable expression he wore earlier.

"It's not that, Santiago. I'm worried about you. Can't friends be worried about each other?" I defend, knowing that it really is about him, and not about the want to know.

"Whatever you say. If you must know, it's family stuff."

Giving him an expectant look, I wait for him to continue. "That's not enough for you?"

"Getting this off your chest might be good for you." My words are more gentle than I even intended them to be, and maybe this is why he finally responds.

"So, a few years ago, I kind of made a *really* stupid decision, and it cost me a lot. If I was considered untrustworthy before, then that was the icing on the cake." Santiago goes on to say that he and his ex-friend were at The Enchanted Ivy and got caught. Even though there were no police or anything, the whole thing left him on thin ice, and he and his friend stopped talking afterwards. And now, Carmen has learned about this, and his older brother has learned the full story. All of which was not supposed to happen.

"And that friend was Alessandro?" I guess. Judging by his expression, I'm right.

"How did you know that?" Santiago questions, his tone letting me know that I'm right.

"Good guess. So what else is going on?"

"As well as that giant mess, Matteo is basically being handed the family business. Which, I actually want. Not for the money or anything, but I love the business idea and everything the business stands for. Matteo wants a part of it, but he's not into any of the logistics, other things like that. He took all of these college classes just to please our parents, and now he's about to take on a whole business." Santiago rushes his words, and the emotion behind them is almost heartbreaking. The pain when he talks about how much this is his dream is something that I've felt before, and I know it all too well.

"Have you told anyone this?"

"Besides you? Not really." He sucks in a breath. "Brooklynn, I'm not trying to be mean, but I don't think you quite realize how much of a disappointment I am to my family. It's not as much my siblings, but my parents really struggle with me. Which is fair, because I used to be more than a little bit difficult. But they can't move past that and see that I'm *really* trying right now."

My heartstrings pull at his words, and if he weren't currently driving, I would pull him into a hug. "Santiago, you're more than your past. As long as you're actually working on becoming a better person, then that's enough. You're more than all of your mistakes and missteps." The words come clearly from me, and I'm not sure how my voice was so steady.

"Brooklynn-"

"Don't argue with me, Santiago. I'm right about this, and you have to believe me. Please believe me."

"But what if no one else can see that I'm moving past who I was?" Santiago questions, as if this is the most important thing.

"Then they're not who you need to be proving yourself to." The answer comes clearly, and I pray with all of my being that Santiago listens to what I'm telling him.

"But I *have* to. You don't understand, Brooklynn."

"I *do* understand. I understand that you think you'll have to make up for your mistakes over and over, and that you think you're less-than because of whatever you did." Sucking in a breath, I continue. "And now I need *you* to understand that I wouldn't be telling you this if I didn't know it to be true. Please hear what I'm saying. You're not a disappointment."

"But what if I am?" Santiago asks, his voice so low that I barely catch his words.

"You're not. I promise you that you're anything but a disappointment. Your family would have to be crazy to think that of you. I may not know you as well as some people do, but everything you've ever been to me is a good—no—*kind* person. I've seen you try your very best whenever I need help. You literally stay up into the early hours of the morning to do things like this for me." Searching for more moments where I've seen him do completely selfless things, a certain one pops into mind. "I saw that guy sit next to your sister the other night, and you dropped everything to get him away from her. You literally left your friends and the rest of the party just so he wasn't near her. You do more selfless things than you know, Santiago."

"But that's different. I have an obligation to both of you. It's easy to do those things without thinking about it." Santiago explains, as though this takes away the selfless things that he's done.

"Just because you have an obligation doesn't mean that what you're doing isn't selfless. Plenty of people are obligated to do things, and they do it to the lowest standard. You go above and beyond for the people in your life."

"Brooklynn, I want to believe you, and I'm going to try to, but please let me have time to process this." Santiago says gently as he slows his car at the front of my house. He slips out of the car and opens my door, and once I'm out with the door shut, I throw my arms around him, pulling Santiago into a hug.

He stiffens for a moment, as if he's unsure of what to do, but within ten seconds, he wraps his arms around me. Santiago's long arms pull me in tighter, the scent of him washing over me.

Santiago's head lowers to my shoulder, and he relaxes his muscles, fully embracing the hug. The air around me stills, and a single tear slips down my cheek at the vulnerability in his body language, and a single thought passes through my mind.

I'm so glad I met Santiago.

"You should get inside," Santiago says gently, moving his body ever so slightly away from mine. I know he's right, but the thought of going inside leaves a pit in my stomach.

"Okay. I'll see you tomorrow at school, right?" Looking hopefully into his eyes, I wait for him to agree. If he doesn't show up to school, I might lose my mind wondering where he is.

"Of course. How else will I keep up my perfect grades?" Santiago asks with a small smile, an attempt at a joke after our *very* emotional conversation.

"I'll see you tomorrow, then," I say, a smile taking over Santiago's face. Something about his smile brings one of my own, and for the life of me, I'm not sure why.

CHAPTER 16

Brooklynn

"You might want to take a look at this, ma'am." My driver says, a hint of worry in his voice as he pulls into the school parking lot. There's no need to ask what he's talking about, because it's glaringly obvious why he's concerned. Most of the parking lot is filled with news outlet vans, reporters, and cameras, all poised at the front entrance.

"Let me call your father. He and the rest of the team need to get on this as soon as possible." Mr Stone says, pulling out his phone in an instant.

"Please do that. I'm going to go inside, but please let my dad know that he should have his lawyers on this."

"Of course, ma'am. Do you need me to walk you in?" His offer tugs at my heartstrings, the pureness in his words comforting.

"I'll be okay, but thank you," I say, sliding the strap for my book bag over my shoulder, exiting the car before Mr. Stone can come open the door for me. There's no need for the paparazzi to start banging down his door.

The yells of excitement from the press drown out all of my thoughts, and as I move through them, I block out all of the lights, questions, microphones, and cameras. I know that my hair and makeup are amazing, so there will be nothing for the headlines to latch onto, except for the fact that I ignored them, making me the villain. Which is totally crazy, because *I'm* the one being followed and harassed, but that doesn't matter. Keeping my eyes on the door, I'm grateful for the *click* of the latch falling back into place, the noise muffled now.

A few students give me quizzical looks as I move through the halls to my locker, but I let it roll off my shoulder. I can deal with strange glances instead of hundreds of reporters waiting to jump on any misstep I make.

I take the wrong turn in my disoriented search for my locker, but I find it after ten minutes of looking. Santiago is waiting for me, and a smile finds its way onto my face when I spot him.

"Hey," I say, opening the lock and switching a few of my books.

"I saw the press." Is Santiago's response, and I stiffen for a moment, wondering how pushy they were with him.

"Were they bad for you, too?" I ask sheepishly, somehow feeling guilty for being the reason they're here.

"Not for me, but Carmen got the brunt of it. She has this modeling thing going on right now, and they realized it was her."

"Oh no. I'm sorry they're here." Sucking in a breath, I push a few curls away from my face. "Is she okay?"

"I think so, but you could talk to her about it if you'd like." Santiago says absently, his attention moving to

Carmen down the hall as she moves books in and out of her locker.

"Wait, you're removing all controlling boyfriend rules and allowing me to talk to your sister?" I tease, finding joy in the way that his face morphs into one of humor.

"Not all of them, but I guess you can have this *privilege*." Santiago teases back, as though I'm not the one who controls this fake relationship.

"Very well, then. See you later," I call out, moving to Carmen's locker down the hall. "Did those crazies get you, too? I'm seriously so tired of them." I say, as I reach her.

"Oh, um, yeah. I guess they're here because there's an actress starting school here?" She says this like a question, and a small smile forms on my lips. For some reason, I'm glad she has no idea who I am. "At least, that's what I caught when I was trying to come in."

"Yeah, that's true," I confirm, debating on the best way to break the news that I'm that actress. "That would be me. Brooklynn Carmine at your service." Extending my hand for a handshake, Carmen's face shifts into one of worry.

"Wow, sorry about that. They said your name like I should recognize you, but I've kind of been trying to stay offline recently." She apologizes, shaking my hand, as though it's a crime for not recognizing me.

I like this girl. Something about these Alvarezes draws me in, and I'm not quite sure why. Carmen and I are definitely going to be friends.

The blaring alarm over the speakers installed throughout the school causes me to stumble, disorienting me for a moment. What in the world is that for? Is there some sort of drill that I'm not aware of?

Students around me start pushing their way down the hallways, and within a few seconds, I'm all alone. That's when. I smell it. The suffocating and headache-inducing odor of smoke.

There's a fire, and I'm not sure where the nearest exit is. There's a fire, and I'm too new here for people to be making sure I get out. There's a fire, and I'm all alone.

Pressure on my head intensifies as I stumble in the direction of the exit. I've always been sensitive to toxic smells, but smoke is on another level. It brings waves of pain down on me, and just as I spot the open doors, I feel a hand on my elbow.

"Brooklynn, come on. You'll be safe out here." Santiago's usually calm voice is clearly stressed, and once we're outside, I lean against one of the cool stone walls, relief washing over me as the fresh air lessens the ache of my head.

"You really can't go-"

"You have to let me go in there! My sister is still in there!" Santiago yells, trying with no avail to enter the school. Carmen is still in there? Oh my gosh. Standing, I do a sweep of all of the students who are currently huddling in groups on the grass, most of them looking traumatized, and a select few looking as though this is an everyday occurrence. Still, no Carmen.

Why is she still in there? Is she hurt? Is she trapped somehow? Thoughts racing and my head pounding, I almost don't notice the security team that comes my way.

"Brooklynn, it's time to go. Your father has requested that you're to be brought home. The whole paparazzi thing on top of this has left him more than anxious." Chris orders. His words sound harsh, but I've been around him long enough to know that this is just how he is. Blunt and point-blank, no time for anything but the truth.

"Do you think I'll be able to stay for just a few more minutes to make sure my friend gets out?" I plead, already knowing what his answer will be.

"I'm sorry, but I take orders from the big man, and right now, that's not you. We need to leave now. The paparazzi are going to have a great day with your current predicament, and we need to be out of here before they get photos of this." Chris says, moving aside so I can walk in front of him on our way out of the yard we're currently in.

Once I'm in the backseat of the SUV that each security team member drives, I send a text to Santiago and ask him to let me know as soon as Carmen is safe and when they've left the school for home.

"Brooklynn, love, we've been so worried about you." Mom exclaims as I walk in the door, her and Dad anxiously looking me up and down for any sign of damage. They both pull me in for a family hug, and I allow myself to embrace their love. They both seem equally shaken, and it's almost comical how they're almost more worried than I am.

"I'm okay, guys. I just need to take a shower and nap, and I'll be okay." I say with false brightness, smiling at them both before taking a few steps to the stairs.

"Okay, but call us if you find any injuries or anything, Brooklynn. We'll go straight to the doctor if there's anything wrong." Mom says firmly, louder than necessary, just to make sure I heard her.

CHAPTER 17

Santiago

Carmen's coming? When did that happen? Peering out the window, I watch her climb into Father's car as they pull out of our driveway. "Hey, did Father say something about Carmen coming along?"

"Yeah, he did. Apparently, Mother is going out to lunch with a friend and doesn't want Carmen to have to be home alone." Matteo answers somewhat stiffly. Cringing, I retreat to my room for a moment, knowing that whatever happens on our car ride into town, it won't be peaceful.

With Carmen finding out about the whole falling out with Alessandro and me, and Matteo realizing that I've been keeping things from him, my house has been *quite* a cheerful place to be.

Even better, I'm going to be in a meeting with my brother, father, Alessandro's father, and Alessandro himself. I've been doing a great job at blocking him out, but I can only hide from my past with him for so long. I really do know that the right thing to do would be to forgive him and move on from our messy falling out, but today isn't the right day.

Something about Brooklynn telling me that my past doesn't define me shifted something in my brain, and it's like I'm a completely different person. Forgiving Alessandro hasn't been something to cross my mind in a long time, but strangely enough, it's been on my mind since that night.

"We really need to get going, Santiago," Matteo calls through my door. Well, I guess it's time to face this problem, too.

"Coming," I call back, taking a steadying breath before following him down the hall and staircase.

An uncomfortable ten minutes pass as we drive, complete silence washing over us. Matteo is just finishing up his inner speech notes before speaking to me. He's always been like this. Composed and thoughtful, the complete opposite of me.

"Santiago, I think I was a little bit unfair with you the other night. I yelled at you, and it was wrong." He finally says. The apology is a surprise, not because Matteo doesn't apologize when he's in the wrong, but it's because he's talking about the other night when the full extent of my bad boy past was revealed.

"Don't-"

"Yes, Santiago. You did your thing, but that shouldn't have provoked me to shout." Matteo says simply, as though it's silly I don't always see eye-to-eye with him. Pressing my lips, I remember that instead of proving what I told him the other night about him is true, I try to focus on the fact that Matteo is a role model, not someone I need to idolize.

"Thank you, Matteo, but I also need to apologize. When

you said that you're not perfect and make mistakes, I shouldn't have said what I did." I say gently, remembering just how mean I was to him.

"What did you say? I really don't remember a lot about then." Matteo asks, and if it were anyone else, I would think that they were just searching for the chance to be a victim again. Not Matteo. He must genuinely not remember, and that hurts even more. How can he move past me being a complete jerk and *forget* about it?

"I told you that you're perfect, and that Mother and Father can't find any flaws with you, and that's why they take all of their frustration out on me." I admit, forcing myself to look his way as I speak, not allowing the shame I feel to take over my body.

"We both said things we regret, but it's behind us now. Don't you think it's time we go back to the old us? When we actually liked each other and didn't argue all of the time?" Matteo questions, and I almost scoff. He always has this way of lowering himself to the other person's level, even if he did nothing wrong.

Matteo was never the reason we started arguing all of the time whenever no one was around. That blame rests heavily on my shoulders, but here Matteo is, taking the burden as though he's played a key part in it, too.

For some reason, this angers me. Why can't he just accept that I'm the problem? Why must he be so good?

"Yeah, Matteo, I'd like that." I say, hoping that my voice doesn't betray me and let on my true feelings. I was honest about the fact that I *do* want to go back to how we used to be, but my feelings about him trying to take part in the burden are still unsettled.

There's nothing more to say now that we're pulling up to Father's building, and just as I'm exiting the car, my eyes catch on an all too familiar vehicle. Alessandro's father's car, to be precise.

For some reason, Brooklynn's face pops into mind as I think about my dislike for Alessandro, and it's not long before I realize why. All of the way through the lobby and up the elevator, I've been trying to figure out why, and now the answer feels as simple as basic math. Brooklyn's dark curls and doe eyes remind me of how she accepted me when I was broken, and reminded me that I'm more than my past. How she forgave and understood me when it felt like nobody would.

Why is this girl coming into my life and shaking up everything I've held on so tightly to? How does she simply, with a few words and an innocent smile, change my perspective on just about everything?

Carmen is shaking Alessandro's hand when we reach Father's personal office and meeting level—which is strange, since he owns the whole building—and for a moment, I swear there's something deeper to Alessandro's smile. No. That's weird, and they've hardly even met before.

Well, besides the time they danced at The Enchanted Ivy because she was alone. At the time, it made my blood boil, but once Carmen explained it, the reasoning was easier to believe.

"All right, let's move into this room across the hall, everyone," Father calls, shaking Mr. Valentino's hand as they already begin talking. So much for trying to sort out my thoughts when these two are already jumping into conversation. Father and Mr. Valentino launch into their business plans, and even though I should be paying attention, my mind wanders to Brooklynn. She was fine after the scare at the school yesterday—there was a small fire, but nothing major—and she's been at home since.

Swallowing hard, the horrible memory of Carmen being inside in all of the smoke resurfaces, and I do everything in my power to forget about it. The guards wouldn't let me go back in—they forcefully held me down—and by just a stroke of luck, Alessandro had run back in the second he came out. He emerged a few minutes later carrying Carmen—not something I'm too fond of—since she was in no position to walk. Apparently, she'd become turned around, and the smoke blowing through the ventilation system made her mind a mess.

I'm not exactly sure why Alessandro went back in, but I do feel like I need to thank him. Yes, I may have unresolved issues with him—which are starting to feel less and less important the more I think about it—but he might have saved my sister's life. The only younger sibling I have, and the only sister I have. The one person I'm supposed to take care of, no matter what.

Carmen being inside as there was a threat to her safety changed something within me, and I swallow again, picturing myself helpless to her being stuck. Glancing over at Alessandro, his eyes aren't on our fathers. Instead, they're on the door, as though he's counting down the minutes until he can leave. Me too. *Me too.*

Alessandro leaves for the restroom after another ten minutes, and a few minutes later, Matteo says that he needs to step out and accept a call. I shoot him a suggestive look, knowing that the call isn't a business one as he's leading on.

His sharp glare reminds me that this might be the only thing I can't poke at in his life.

Matteo is serious about his woman, and to be honest, I would be too if I were the one getting a second chance at love. When Matteo initially started dating back in high school, it was something our parents were more than against, which is why he kept his relationship a secret. When I—stupid thirteen-year-old Santiago—found out and started talking about it during dinner, not knowing they were against it, that ended the relationship with his girlfriend.

"Santiago, since you're the only one in here, please sign this as a witness for our agreement," Father says exasperatedly, and I notice that Alessandro and Matteo are both still gone. Resisting the urge to roll my eyes, I take the pen Mr. Valentino is extending towards me, and sign my name on the small line a few spaces below his and Father's. To be honest,I don't even know what agreement they just made, but it doesn't worry me too much.

Alessandro opens the door and quickly takes his seat again, looking...excited about something, and I chalk it up to him being excited to leave this stuffy meeting. Honestly, it would be great to leave right about now, but here they go again with their talking.

"Come on, you'll have fun." Brooklynn mock pleads through the phone, her voice excited.

"But don't you think it's just a little bit...late?" I ask, the idea of spending time with Brooklynn is alluring, but her plans are…unique.

"Of course not. Searching for seashells is one of my traditions this time of year. Tonight is supposed to be a full moon." Brooklynn rattles off. "And, tomorrow is that party, with the premiere stuff the day after. This is kind of my last chance for a while. If you don't want to come, I'll drive the forty-five minutes in the dark myself, and I'll walk the beach alone. Sleep well, Santiago."

"Stop, stop. I'm going to come." I say, reaching for a jacket. "I'll be at your house in a few minutes."

"Perfect! See you then." Brooklynn exclaims, and I notice that I walked right into her 'trap'. Smiling, I hang up, knowing full well that I don't mind agreeing with her plans. That's kind of always how our relationship has been. She's been the mastermind, and I just follow along. It's different than any other friendship I've had, where I'm always the leader, and I don't mind it one bit.

I slip on my hoodie and find appropriate beach shoes, snagging my car keys off my desk, and walk out of my door. It's late enough that I probably shouldn't be leaving, but just to be on the safe side, I use the hallway window, knowing that I can use the house keys when I come back if needed.

Once I'm on the road, I try to picture Brooklynn walking along the night shore, collecting seashells and listening to the soft lapping of waves, but I can't picture it. It's probably much warmer back in Los Angeles this time of year, and since this is the first time Brooklynn is going to visit one of our East Coast beaches, I want it to be perfect.

"Oh my gosh, you really got here quickly. You weren't

speeding, were you?" Brooklynn teases, sliding into the car before I can even shift it into park. "To the beach!"

Smiling, I let my foot off the brake. "Of course not. Let's not forget that I happen to have most of the roads around here memorized and know every shortcut this town has to offer."

"Really, now? I'll hold you to that, Santiago." Brooklynn asks suspiciously. "I can't wait to get to the beach, by the way. Back in Las Angeles, we went all the time, but since we've been here, I haven't been once. It's pretty much a crime against humanity, in my book."

"Is it now?" I tease, loving how she is both bubbly and happy, but also extremely funny and sarcastic.

"Absolutely. Have you never heard of ocean therapy?" Brooklynn questions, sounding more than serious.

"I can't say I have, what is it?"

"How would I know? I just made it up, hoping to get my point across." Brooklynn teases, crossing her legs on the seat, her sandals falling to the floorboard. Her black leggings hug her skin, and her pink short-sleeved shirt is not much better.

"You're kind of convincing, you know?" I tease, knowing that I'm talking about more than just this situation.

"Am I? That's good to know." She says, her hair—as much of it as can fit in a hair tie—bobs in the bun she's thrown it in, the other curls bouncing around her face and neck.

"Absolutely." I answer with complete certainty, knowing that not many people would be able to convince me to do half of the stuff she's pulled me along for.

"I'll keep that card in my back pocket, then," Brooklynn replies smugly, leaning against the window, her brown-gold skin glowing in the window reflection. For a moment, the desire to pull the car over and just marvel at the beauty Brooklynn possesses passes over me, and I blink rapidly, erasing the thought from my brain. Where did that even come from? I see her all of the time and never have thoughts like that. "Oh, I can see one of the carnival rides from here!" Brooklynn squeals as we drive into the small town of Rockdale.

"We'll park a little bit away from there, but if you'd like to, we can ride a few of them." I offer, Brooklynn's excitement wearing off on me.

"That would be fun, but we have a strict mission tonight. Seashells, not carnival rides." Brooklynn replies firmly, as though she's trying to remind herself of this, too. I'll admit that her rejection stings just a little bit, but I chalk it up to me wanting to ride one of the rides, not to Brooklynn rejecting my idea.

"Okay, then." I say, parking my car and climbing out, Brooklynn exiting before I can even get halfway around the car.

"Seashells, here we come," Brooklynn says, and I notice the small pouch that she has tied to her wrist, and only now do I realize how much of an operation this will be. This is like a sport to her or something. Brooklynn continues walking to the shore, and a second later, she turns to my still figure. "Well, you're coming, aren't you?" She calls back, waving her arm. Smiling, I take off in a jog to catch up to her.

CHAPTER 18

Brooklynn

Smiling, I scoop up the perfect flat shell, the color almost indistinguishable in the moonlight. One of the main reasons that this is something I only do at night is because there's so much I can't see that I normally would if it were daylight. Now, I rely on the pattern and size of a shell to tell me its beauty, not the color. "Santiago, feel this one," I demand, shoving the perfect shell into his hand, sand rubbing against my skin, causing tingling to shoot up my arm. Weird.

"It's...nice?" Santiago offers, and I almost recoil at the lack of admiration in his voice.

"Since you're so ungrateful, hand me that right now." I gasp, snatching my shell away from him. I gently place it in my bag, the first of many shells I plan to collect tonight. "Now that your hands are empty, please do carry my sandals. I can't really search with only one hand, and apparently I'm dealing with an amateur shell collector, so this is better for both of us." I tease, not at all expecting Santiago's fingers to wrap around mine for a moment as he takes the straps of my sandals.

"Can I ask you a question?" Santiago asks a few minutes later, and I almost don't hear him over the lapping of the waves. My feet sink into the wet sand as we walk, the occasional cool water washing my feet.

"Sure," I'll say with a shrug, reaching down to pick up the tiny shell that just poked my foot.

"Why is your last name Carmine? It's Italian, right?" Santiago questions. "I don't think either of your parents are Italian, and I'm pretty sure you're their child. Seriously, you resemble them both so much."

"Thanks, Santiago." Taking a breath, I rub the round shell in my hand. "My dad was adopted. The family that adopted him—my grandparents—are Italian, though."

"Oh, sorry for-"

"No, it's fine. It's not really a secret. My grandparents adopted because they weren't able to have a baby of their own. Funny enough, only three months after adopting my dad, they found out they were pregnant with twins." Smiling, I drop the shell into my pouch. "They had six more kids after my dad and the twins, so I have a *lot* of aunts and uncles. Cousins, too."

"Wow, nine kids is a lot." Santiago comments.

"Yeah, my grandparents are pretty great. They were hesitant when my dad started acting, but they've never been anything but supportive of him, and now me."

"It sounds like it." Santiago reaches down and hands me a shell, and for some reason, that tugs at something deep in my heart, but I can't figure out why. The jagged edges are sharp on my fingertips, but I run my finger along them anyway, the edge just dull enough not to cut into flesh. "Where did Brooklynn come from? Why did your parents choose it?"

"Actually, my parents didn't," I say with a smile, the dark shadows of Santiago's face twisting into confusion.

"What do you mean?"

"Well, I guess my mom kind of did, but not really. My dad was convinced that I was a boy—they didn't learn my gender until I was born—and my mom was convinced I was a girl. They both made their baby names based on the gender they were certain of, and decided that if they were wrong, the other one would get to choose my name. Well, when I came out a girl, my mom felt bad for my dad because he wasn't going to have a chance to name a baby, and combined some of the names they each had picked out."

"That's actually really sweet, but had they already decided that they wouldn't have more kids?" Santiago questions, curiosity obvious in his tone.

"My mom has a health problem, and they were lucky to even get pregnant with me, so they knew that the chances were slim to none. Now they tease me about how God knew they could only handle one of me, but I know for a while that back in their earlier marriage, it put a strain on them. They seem happy, though." I say, carefully calculating how my words will seem, knowing that anyone else would store this information away for a rainy media day. Telling Santiago these things doesn't worry me, and I'm thankful for the opportunity to speak freely with someone.

"Wow, I'm really dragging all of the insider family information out of you this evening, aren't I?" Santiago teases, trying to lighten the mood. It's not that the mood has dampened, but it definitely feels heavier.

"Apparently so. Maybe you should reconsider your plans and move into detective work." I tease back, knowing that Santiago would never drop his position at his father's business.

"Maybe. But, the condition would be that you're my detective partner." Santiago says, his voice changing into something a little bit deeper.

"And why would that be?"

"You're a convincing person. You could convince a criminal to plead guilty to every one of his crimes, all while doing it willingly." Santiago answers, his words teasing, but his words sounding more serious than he's sounded in a while.

"Maybe, but my talents are in front of a camera, with the entire world ready to pounce on any media that gets released. I'm not too sure that hanging out with criminals all day is something I'm interested in."

"Probably so, but a career change might still be arrangeable at your age." Santiago teases, his comment taking me aback.

"A career change? How would that even be possible at this point? Not that I want to, of course, but wouldn't there be casting agents knocking down my door every day if I were to just disappear one day?" I question, the logistics of it fascinating me.

"Honestly, probably so." The cold water that comes in a large wave rises all the way to my knees, and my body immediately shivers from the cold. "Here, have this,"

Santiago says immediately, pulling off his hoodie and offering it to me.

"Oh, I can't take that. You'll be cold, now." I refuse, shaking my head. The idea of wearing his warm jacket is tempting, but I can't just force him to give it to me. Well, I could...

"Yes, you can. I'll be perfectly fine. Let's not forget that you're the newbie here, and I've lived in this cooler climate a lot longer." Santiago argues back, moving his hoodie even closer to me.

"Goodness, just give it to me, then." I huff, secretly happy. I really am cold, and I've never been to a beach this chilly. There wasn't exactly a proper clothing guide, and I just picked the first few items my eyes landed on in my closet. Sliding the jacket over my head, I'm immediately warmed. Sure, the hem of it reaches mid-thigh and the sleeves are long enough to easily cover my hands, but it's warm and smells amazing. The hood is another matter, and with my hair in the bun that it's in, more than half of my hair is spilling from it.

"See, you really did need it," Santiago says smugly, wrapping his arm around my shoulder. Something about this gesture feels completely normal, but something about it also feels foreign. His arm is honestly a little bit heavy—probably all of the muscles I've gotten a glimpse of on a few rare occasions—but I don't mind. I do, however, mind the strange sensation in my pulse that feels as though it's not working the same way it was five minutes ago.

"Maybe," I finally say. "Hey! Look at the shooting star!" I gasp, jumping to point at the star. Santiago grunts lightly as my shoulder jostles him, but he doesn't say anything. "Did you see it?"

"Yeah, I was making my wish." Santiago says lightly, and I do a double-take.

"You believe in that?"

"Not really, but it's still something that reminds me of being a child. Matteo used to take Carmen and me outside way past our bedtime, and lay blankets out in the yard to watch the stars." My heartstrings tug a little as I imagine a young Santiago with his siblings.

"That's so cute. How old were you when he did that?" I'm not sure why I ask, but for some reason, I want my imagination to be as clear as possible.

"I was probably six or seven. That would have made Carmen somewhere around four. Honestly, I doubt she even remembers it." Santiago answers with a chuckle, and my picture broadens at the thought of a tiny Carmen running after her older brothers.

"Aw, that's literally so adorable. Sometimes I wish I had siblings, but I try to remember that this is God's plan, you know? Hearing stories about you and yours does kind of make me jealous." I admit, the words tumbling from my mouth. "And by the way, I've never told anyone that before, so feel special."

"There have been a few times where I've wished that I were an only child, but those are rare moments, now. I'm not really sure what I'd do without them." Santiago says softly, and it's only now that I realize that we're still standing still. "I think we should get back. Tomorrow is that party, and the next day is your premiere."

"Ugh, don't remind me." I joke, leaning into his side a

little bit more, a yawn escaping me. In the distance, the hoops and hollers of teenagers at the carnival carry over to us, and I smile. The water is just quite enough for the sounds of the music to carry, and I don't ever want to leave. "Are you nervous?" The question pops out of me, and I'm not sure why I'm even asking.

"For what? The party?"

"No, the premiere. What if something goes wrong? Or what if people hate me now that Kai's lies are floating around the internet?"

"First of all, nothing will go wrong, and secondly, if people hate you—which they don't—then let them hate." Santiago says simply.

"I guess so."

"What's that supposed to mean?" Santiago questions again, and I resist the urge to roll my eyes.

"My father is Xander Carmine, and he has the whole industry willing to do anything for his stamp of approval. People are now spinning this too make it seem as though I was the one threatening Kai and telling him not to go to the press with the 'truth', because the minute my dad speaks about Kai, it will be over for him." I say matter-of-factly. And then something truly unexpected happens. Santiago laughs. *Laughs.* "What's so funny?"

"I can't believe how hard they're trying to spin this on you. They seem to only see that jerk with rose-colored glasses, and it's so infuriating that it's humorous. How are they so stupid to not see how bad Kai is?" Santiago says. At least someone gets this.

"I completely agree. How could *I* be the problematic one here? I'm barely seventeen years old and have no intentions of hurting someone. Also, don't they think that it's a little bit crazy that in this fantasy, where I'm the bad guy, Kai played no villain roles?"

"How can they just so easily believe what he's feeding them. It actually amazes me to see how against you they are."

"Tell me about it, Santiago. While I agree that Kai can be more than a little bit convincing at times, *someone* should be able to sniff out the truth on this one." I huff, wrapping my arms around Santiago's arm, leaning against it as we walk.

"We really should go," Santiago says with a sigh, turning us to walk back to his car.

"We should." I echo, each step taking more and more effort as tiredness crashes over me.

The soft sand crunches under my bare feet as we walk, and I appreciate how Santiago deliberately moves us away from the glass and sharp rocks, as though he has night vision or something. "Here, make sure your feet are in." Santiago says gently as he closes the passenger door for me. What a gentleman.

"Tomorrow's party will be fun, right?" I ask a few minutes into our drive, the silence sending chills up and down my neck.

"It should be, as long as you hang out with the right people." Santiago says somewhat ominously.

"And that's supposed to mean..." I trail off in the hopes that he'll elaborate.

"It just means that..." Santiago sucks in a deep breath of air and pauses as he changes lanes. "You should be careful about who you hang out with. There's this guy there, the one that I had an encounter with a few weeks ago, and I really don't trust him."

"So, stay clear of any and all enemies of Santiago's?" I tease.

"Something like that." He answers with a smile. There's something else brewing under his expression, but I'm too tired to try to decipher it.

"Noted. Just remember that the day after tomorrow is the day we leave, and I'm going to need you at my manager's office early in the morning. Probably seven?" I say this as a question, because I'm not quite sure of the exact time.

"I'll be there. Should there be anything I need to be aware of? Is there some sort of boyfriend protocol that I need to follow?" Santiago asks, sounding like he genuinely means his question. My mind stops for a moment when he leaves out the fake boyfriend part, but surely he just forgot to add that part because he's tired or something.

"I mean, this is kind of the first time I've ever had to deal with something like this, but I'm assuming it'll be pretty easy. I'm kind of learning as I go." I answer honestly, since I'm not too sure about what else to say.

"How often do you think relationships in the rich and famous world are fake, and entirely publicity stunts?" Santiago asks, breaking through the silence a few minutes later.

"Probably a lot. My parents kind of kept me out of that world when I was growing up, so I'm not too sure." I say, running my hands through my hair. "That's kind of the reason we moved. So that I could still do my acting but not be under the influence of that world."

"Really? I thought it was about your dad slowing down his career."

"That's kind of the story he's going with," I say lightly,

knowing how much of a sacrifice the whole move has been for him.

"So, why is the premiere happening here? Shouldn't it be in Los Angeles?" Santiago asks, his questions still coming. I appreciate the effort to converse, but seriously, I'm tired..

"It's actually in New York City. We're taking my father's private plane to get there." I say rather nonchalantly, only now realizing that my words sound kind of snobby. "Which is super amazing, by the way. I completely recognize that having a father so famous isn't normal." I add on, sounding even worse than before.

"Relax, Brooklynn. I didn't think you were being rude or anything. You don't have to worry about that with me." Santiago says gently, a light laugh following his words.

"Thanks. I guess I'm slightly on edge with the whole Kai thing. It has kind of been a lot." I admit, knowing that I've been playing it off as though it doesn't bother me.

"Listen, what Kai did was wrong, but you shouldn't let that change the way you are. He shouldn't be able to put his dirty hands on your personality." Santiago states, and for a moment, I just watch him in amazement. Who knew this misunderstood "bad boy" gives the best advice and knows how to give the perfect pep-talk? Not me.

"Wow, that was pretty solid. I might just need to look into hiring you as my personal pep-talk person or something. Is that a job you can hire for?"

"It probably is, but I promise I'm not as wise as you're making me out to be. I just know the truth from the lies, and know that you're not at fault for this. Kai really tried to bury you, which is totally not cool." Santiago replies, as though this is a normal conversation.

"I know deep down that you're right, but sometimes it's almost easier to just imagine that none of this was him," I confess, twirling a few curls around my finger. "I was in my first two movies with him. For the last year and a half, I've trusted him. I didn't realize he liked me until right when I rejected him, so he knows things about me that I don't just go announcing to the world."

"What does he know about you that I don't?" Santiago says, like this is his only takeaway. It both causes me to roll my eyes, but also smile at his straightforwardness.

"A lot of things. You're forgetting that I was in a relationship with him for a long time. A work relationship, but a relationship, still." I say, as though Santiago is just silly for asking.

"Aren't I in a relationship with you?"

"A *fake* relationship."

"Same thing."

"Is not."

"Is too." Sighing from his persistence, I press my warm cheek to the cold, dark window, a yawn escaping me. Somehow, I'm both tired and fully awake, but also nervous and excited. All of these emotions pretty much sum up the last few days.

"Okay, then." I finally say, shrugging my shoulders as the reason behind Santiago's persistence nags at my mind. Why is he so determined? A smile forms on my lips as I realize that's one of my favorite qualities of his. His determination is quite endearing, if I'm being honest. Santiago doesn't say anything else for the rest of the drive, but neither do I. Usually, I feel the need to fill silence with conversation, but right now, I'm absolutely content to ride in the quiet.

"Thanks for letting me tag along." Santiago says as he closes the car door behind me. I glance down at the pouch that's resting in my hand.

"Thank *you* for taking me. It was a lot more fun with you there." I reply honestly, my eyes meeting Santiago's. His dark eyes stare into mine, and for the strangest reason, it feels like they're pulling me into him.

"No, I was just the driver and bodyguard. I'm glad you found some good shells, though." He pauses, blinking rapidly for a moment, as though the gears in his brain are spinning. "I'll see you tomorrow at the party, Brooklynn."

"Yeah, I'll see you then," I reply with a smile, pursing my lips for a moment as I consider my next move. "Have a nice night, Santiago," I say, pulling him into a quick hug. Santiago tightens his arms around me for a moment before pulling away.

"Good night, Brooklynn." And with that, he turns to get in his car. My insides feel warm as I walk through the gates and to the front door, but for the life of me, I can't figure out why.

Brooklynn

My red dress flows behind me as I enter The Enchanted Ivy, and if it weren't for my thumping heart, I would be admiring it a lot more. As I search the crowds of people for Santiago, I spot Carmen and Alessandro talking quietly, and the memory of her becoming flustered when I asked her about him in class a few weeks ago rushes back.

Oh my gosh. They're totally together. There's no other explanation for the expressions on their faces. I can tell that whatever they're talking about is serious, but they're too far away to make out any words. Finally catching sight of Santiago, I rush forward, desperate to tell him my theory. I know that he's had past issues with Alessandro, but that's not why I'm bringing it up.

"I almost thought you decided not to attend tonight's party." Santiago says as I approach him, an easy smile on his face.

"What? Me? Never. I was simply a little bit late because

there was a shoe incident." I reply, raising my eyebrows as I take in his expression.

"And that was?" He asks.

"Well, if you must know, I was coming down the stairs, and I tripped, causing one of my heels to break. Yes, *break*." I say, relaying the awful events of earlier. "I literally almost died. My dad just happened to be coming down, too. Otherwise..." I shudder at the horrible incident that would have occurred otherwise.

"Okay, that does actually sound pretty bad. I'm glad you're okay, though. Imagine going down the red carpet on a stretcher." Santiago teases, but true gratitude is in his eyes.

"Oh my gosh, don't even say that. Can you imagine? I would rather just miss the whole thing and never act again if it came to that." I gasp, the horrendous vision that Santiago just created replaying in my mind.

"It would be the talk of the town, though. Maybe the gossip articles would be too interested in that story rather than the one Kai fabricated." Santiago says lightly, obviously trying to reassure me now.

"You're right about that one. Maybe it *would* be enough to leave that story in the past." I muse, the thought entertaining. "Especially if I just got up and started walking after I acted like I was bedridden."

"Hey, now. Let's not actually get a crazy idea like that." Santiago teases, like I was actually considering it.

"Of course not, silly. I was just thinking about it. You have to admit that something like that would be absolutely hilarious." I reply, rolling my eyes at the absurdity of it. "Really, Santiago, I really wouldn't be caught dead rolling down the red carpet in a stretcher. You would be a billion times taller than me, then."

"Aren't I already a lot taller than you?" Santiago teases, laughter in his eyes.

"Of course *that's* your concern. Seriously, Santiago, you're quite something."

"Brooklynn, do you mind coming over here for a minute?" My dad calls out before Santiago can respond, and only now do I realize how it just felt like Santiago and I were the only people in this room. I completely forgot there were people all around us.

"I'll find you in a little bit," Santiago says, his eyes motioning to my dad before turning and walking away.

"Okay, that sounds good. I shouldn't be too long." I reply, quickly stepping to Dad.

"Brooklynn, I would love for you to meet the Valentino family." He says, gesturing to a woman, her son, and her husband. I shake the woman's hand before turning to the boy, and my hand freezes for a moment. This is Alessandro. Quickly righting myself, I shake his hand politely.

"Oh, Alessandro, just look at her dress." His mother says, and I can hear that tone that mothers use whenever they're trying to convey something else. Judging by the way she's eyeing me and the fact that Santiago seems to have no clue about whatever is going on between Carmen and Alessandro, I take a well-educated guess that their relationship is a secret.

"Yes, Mother. It's quite nice." Alessandro agrees, his heart not sounding in it. As soon as I try to step away, Dad gently rests his hand on my arm, and I realize that I'm being pulled into an hour-long conversation that will certainly bore me to death.

Ten or so minutes pass by before Alessandro excuses himself, and I wish to do the same. Another ten minutes pass by, and I find a break in the conversation to excuse myself, using the reason of needing water. Not my finest moment, I'll admit, but one can only listen to Mrs. Valentino talk about how amazing her son is. Not that I have anything against Alessandro, but I kind of have a thing against bragging, and that seems to be the only thing his mom knows how to do.

After thirty minutes of just hanging around and doing nothing, I start to question if Santiago forgot about his promise to meet me. No, he wouldn't do that. Right?

Another thirty minutes pass, and by now, I'm upset. Why would Santiago just forget about me? Sweeping my eyes across the room, for a moment, I think I've finally spotted him, but when the man turns, it becomes obvious that this is his brother, Matteo. While their looks aren't strikingly similar, their tall figures, dark hair, and sharp features are definitely dead giveaways that they're brothers. Matteo bends his head to speak to someone, and I shift my eyes from him, but there's still no Santiago.

The rest of my evening is spent sticking by Mom's side as she chats with groups of women, but my eyes never stop searching for Santiago. I regret leaving my phone at the house, because otherwise, I would just text him and ask where he is.

Just before leaving, I survey the room one last time for Santiago, and realize that while he's not here, neither is Carmen or Alessandro. Did something happen to them, or is it just a coincidence? Suddenly feeling very stupid, I only now consider something bad happening, and that being the cause of him being absent. Wow, I'm such a horrible person for just automatically assuming that whatever happened has to do with me.

The entire drive home, I try to reassure myself that maybe Santiago just got busy, but now that the thought of him not being okay is plaguing my mind, it's hard. There's a text from him when I get home, and while it's short, it's to the point. It says that someone needed him, and he had to leave early. It also mentions that he'll still be on time tomorrow.

I type back a quick response, letting him know that I hope the person who needed help is okay, and that I can't wait to see him tomorrow. Maybe a bit over-the-top, but maybe he's having a hard evening and needs a pick-me-up. Not that he'll be overjoyed to receive that message or anything, but maybe it will bring him a quick smile. That's all.

This is quite the predicament to be in, I muse, sliding into pajama shorts and a sweater, flopping into bed. Why am I this concerned about Santiago when he's literally just my friend? Well, fake boyfriend, too. Besides that, why am I this overcome with thoughts about him? I'm never like this.

"What happened to you?" I screech, my eyes moving up and down Santiago's body as he enters the elevator next to me in Marie's office building. The purple-blue bruises mark a good portion of his face and all of his hands. I reach out a hand to press it to his chest, and he winces and pulls away. "Santiago, are you okay? What happened?"

"It's kind of a long story, but let's just say that last night didn't go as planned." He answers dryly.

"Well, I can see that," I reply, placing my hands on my hips, staring intently at him hard enough that one would think I'm trying to get rid of the bruising with just my eyes.

"So, are you excited for tonight's big reveal?" He teases, as though we're going to just move past the elephant in the room. Well, bruising in the elevator.

"The big reveal of what? My makeup team will be taking care of this, don't worry." I say, disbelief in my tone. Does he really think he'll get past all of the people in charge of getting me red-carpet-ready will just let him slide by them?

"No, I meant the dating thing. I assumed that your people might want to do something about this." Santiago says easily, motioning to his face and hands.

"Santiago, what is wrong with you? I'm genuinely asking." I demand, fully meaning it. How does he just show up the morning of a movie premiere looking like this and cracking jokes?

"Well-" He doesn't get to finish his sentence because the doors are opening, and Marie's face is greeting us. Her gaze goes from expectant, to confused, to horrified, in the matter of one second.

"Oh, well, good morning to you, Brooklynn. I'm assuming this is the man who was supposed to help with our problems?" She says, as though not quite believing that this man is going to actually help.

"Yeah, this would be Santiago," I reply, my voice higher-pitched than normal, her scrutinizing gaze enough to tell me all that I need to know.

"Hello, ma'am." Santiago greets Marie, extending a hand out to her. To Marie's credit, she does shake it, but the way her eyes take in the bruises displays her true feelings.

"Hello, Santiago. Lovely meeting you." She manages, quickly looking over at me. "Why don't we all visit my office and take a quick look at what we have planned and what we need to do before this evening."

"Yes, of course," I say, falling into step behind her, Santiago right at my side. "You really need to be on your best behavior, Santiago." I hiss, half-joking, but half meaning it. Whatever he's gotten himself into will not fly with Marie, and he hasn't met the full force of this woman yet.

"Okay, do you mind telling me where you got all of... those?" Marie questions once we're all seated in her office.

"The bruises?" Santiago asks, as though she would be asking about something else.

"Yes, those."

"It's kind of a long story, but more than that, it's personal." Santiago says, deflecting her question in the perfect way.

"Well then, that's fine. We can move past them as long as you can promise that whatever created those won't be on my red carpet tonight." Marie starts, the slightest of smiles appearing on her face. "Might I say, you're going to be perfect for this job. You deflected that question easily but firmly. That's what you need to do from now on."

"Thank you, ma'am. Now, what else do I need to know?"

CHAPTER 20

Santiago

By the time Marie is done giving me the run-down on everything I'm supposed to do, there's the slightest bit of worry within me. Basically, there are a thousand things that could go wrong, and it's my job to make sure none of those things happen.

"One last question, if you don't mind," I say as Marie shuffles a few papers. She nods, barely glancing up as she does so. "Let's just say there's a moment in which I'll have to introduce myself, what am I supposed to do? I know we've said that I'm supposed to pretty much be nameless, but what if that doesn't work?"

"Then you're allowed to say your name—I would definitely leave out your last name—but you'll remind people that this evening is for Brooklynn," Marie answers smoothly, and I nod.

"Of course it's about her, I was just wondering what I should do in that exact predicament."

"I have a feeling tonight will be just fine so long as you both stick to this plan. I've crafted this down to the tiniest detail, and I just need you to follow my script. This is about your movie, and changing the course of the media's attention." Marie says, her tone isn't rude, but I can tell that the light frustration in her voice is a product of the stress she's under.

"I understand, Marie." Brooklynn finally speaks up, and for a moment, she's wearing an expression that I've never seen before, her big eyes opening and closing quickly.

"You want to do this, right?" The words tumble from my mouth, and Brooklynn's reaction is one of surprise and curiosity.

"What?"

"You want to do this whole red-carpet and premiere? You want me there?"

"Of course, I want you there." Brooklynn sputters, as though the idea is laughable. "I can't do this without you there, Santiago. Don't tell me you're bailing on me last minute." She says, her voice rising a few octaves.

"No, of course I'm not bailing on you. I'm just..." I trail off as I try to find the right words. "I don't really know how much of a contract you have, but if you don't want to do this, then I don't want you to feel pressured."

"Oh, well, thank you. It's not in my contract, but there's no way I'm missing this, especially because of what Kai has done to my reputation." Brooklynn finally says, crossing her arms. "And I definitely need you there. I'm going to be a wreck. You know that, right?" She adds, the panic in her eyes growing with each word.

"Okay, okay, let's not go that far, now. How about we get you both on a plane and you can talk on the way there." Marie interrupts, seemingly realizing that nothing good is going to come from Brooklynn going into a panic.

"You're not coming?" Brooklynn gasps, and I have to admit that Marie not coming sounds extremely odd.

"I am, don't worry. My plane leaves in two hours, though. Yours, however, leaves in," she checks her watch before looking up again, "an hour. You need to get to that airport now."

"Oh my gosh, we have to go!" Brooklynn exclaims, grabbing my arm and pulling me out of the office and to the elevator. "My parents are going to be there, so you'll get to meet them on the plane."

"What a fun, family bonding moment." I muse, leaning against the elevator wall as it descends.

"What's that supposed to mean?" Brooklynn questions, bracing her hand on the rail.

"I just meant that it will be quite the first conversation, right? Imagine you had a daughter and the first time you meet her boyfriend, it's because she needed someone to help draw attention away from her reputation that her ex co-star is trying to destroy."

"Well, that's one way to look at it, I guess. But you're not technically my boyfriend." As she says this, my face stays completely emotionless, but inside, I wince a little. As fake as this whole scheme is supposed to be, my heart is doing a great job of forgetting that. Which is completely silly, but try telling it that. It's clear that Brooklynn doesn't see it the same way, because whenever I slip up, she's quick to correct me.

"Santiago!" Brooklynn screams, launching herself towards me as there's a giant shake in the elevator, the whole thing completely stopping

CHAPTER 21

Brooklynn

"Don't freak out, but we're stuck here." Santiago's words are muffled due to my head being pressed to his chest, and my arms wrapped tightly around his middle, but I hear the message loud and clear.

"No, no, no. This can't be happening." I whisper, tears pricking at the corner of my eyes. "Santiago, don't say that. Surely there's a mistake."

"Are you okay? Because we're one hundred percent stuck in here." Santiago answers, his voice almost calm.

"Am I okay? Santiago, this is one of my biggest fears right here. There's a way out, right?"

"Well, there's no way out, but we'll just call someone. Here, give me your phone and I'll call your manager and let her know that we need maintenance." Santiago replies coolly, reaching his hand into my purse as he speaks. "Can you unlock this?"

"It's four, two, five." I manage, my fingers digging into Santiago's shirt. "I'm really claustrophobic, can't do this much longer without a panic attack, so the sooner, the better."

"Oh, well, that's not a problem. I'm sure there will be someone here soon." He says, clicking dial, bringing the phone to his ear to relay all of the information to Marie. "You don't have maintenance on call? Well, when can you get someone here? Okay, okay, I understand." I hear the noise my phone makes when the call is disconnected, and my chest squeezes a little bit tighter.

"She can't get us out." I infer, my heart pumping harder and harder.

"It's not that she can't get us out; rather, she just doesn't have the right people on hand right now, so we have to get comfy for at least forty-five minutes."

"*Forty-five minutes!*" I shriek, my breathing coming out more and more erratic.

"Maybe a little bit sooner, but that's the estimate. Why don't we just sit down and talk?" Santiago says reassuringly, his words anything but that.

"Talk about how I'm about to die? Sure, let's do that." I say humorously, sinking to the floor next to Santiago. "This is genuinely one of my worst fears, Santiago. You don't get it."

"I don't get it, but I'm also here for you. Why don't we talk about Summer's Mirage? How did you get casted?" Santiago questions, completely changing the topic.

"Well, I finally told my parents that I absolutely needed to start acting, so they helped me look for good roles to audition for, and when this one opened, I sent in some videos of me acting, and I was accepted." I try to remember all of the details from that time in my life, but a lot of them are fuzzy, since my life became incredibly busy right around them.

"So they just immediately knew that you were the girl for the job?"

"I guess so. Within a week, they let me know that I would be playing the main lead in Summer's Mirage." I say with a smile, remembering how excited I'd been when I received the phone call. "Then I came to the office with my dad's lawyers and my parents, where I signed the contract."

"If it was filmed last year, why is it only now being released? Didn't you film Our Story this year, and it's already out?" Santiago questions, wrapping his arm around my shoulder. I lean into his touch, resting my head on his arm.

"I don't know, actually." Chewing my lip, the reasoning doesn't come to me. "There might have been an issue with the producer leaving after all of the filming was over, but I honestly didn't care. My dad's lawyers looked into it, but I was just so excited to be in a movie that the release being pushed back didn't matter."

"Wow, I don't think I would've been the same way." Santiago admits.

"Yeah, I don't think I could now, but at the time, I was just a little bit naive." Smiling, I twist one of the rings on my thumb. "You're going to witness my first acting job, so you have to promise that you won't laugh or anything. My acting has improved considerably since then."

"I doubt your acting abilities will be the forefront thing in my mind tonight." Santiago says with a chuckle, his fingers running up and down my arm as he speaks.

"What's going to be the most interesting thing, then? You know, besides the ruining of my reputation, of course."

I tease, making light of the pretty bad situation my career is in.

"Just not messing up will be taking up a lot of my brain, and watching out for that guy is also something."

"Trust me, dear, we're going to be seeing a *lot* of Kai. In fact, most of the night is going to be spent with him. That's the unfortunate part of being co-stars." I say with a resigned sigh, the thought of having to be around Kai for hours is tiring me already.

"Yeah, I guess that's kind of how it works, but I'm not happy about it." Santiago finally responds, his tone sounding frustrated. "I seriously don't get how he can get away with all of this."

"You're telling me." I huff. "And all of the obsessive Kai fans will be there, with all of the reporters shoving microphones in my face, asking about why I was so unprofessional."

"How are you going to dodge all of those questions?" Santiago inquires curiously.

"Marie gave me a few different responses, but the gist of them all is that we should focus on the movie and stay away from personal life. Which, of course, will only deter them for so long, but with you being there, and the probability of Rachel being there, people will be more interested in that story."

"Marie is really good at coming up with the answer to every scenario, huh?"

"Very. I can't think of a time when she didn't have the perfect words ready. It's a superpower or something, I'm telling you." I can feel the nod of his head in response. "By the way, how does your family feel about this little plan of ours?" I ask, just now realizing that I have no idea if they're going to despise me after this.

"Honestly, I just told my parents this morning that I'm going to be going with you, and at this point, they're kind of used to anything with me." Santiago says bluntly.

"So they're not wondering why you're just going to a movie premiere with an actress they know nothing of?" I question, his answer not really convincing. Yes, he sounded sure of himself, but really, his parents don't care?

"Not at all."

"Well, that's a little bit interesting." I finally say, not knowing what else would be a good response.

"Why? You already know what they think of me." Santiago says this as nonchalantly as possible, but it still makes me pause. Yeah, he said that they're disappointed in him for his previous wrongdoings, but surely they're not holding a grudge or something, right?

"I guess I didn't know that it was to that extent. I think if my child were to come to me and say that they were going to a red carpet premiere, I would want to know just a little bit more. Maybe that's just me, though." I finally reply, my words sounding harsher than the intended delivery. Santiago doesn't respond, and I worry that I've hurt his feelings. "Listen, I wasn't trying to be mean, I-"

"It's okay, Brooklynn. I know what you were trying to say, and I agree with you." Santiago's words aren't exactly clipped, but they're definitely surface-level. Now I've gone and done it.

"I'm sorry, Santiago. I really didn't mean to sound rude or judgmental, even though I know that's how it sounded." I try again, needing Santiago to know my true intentions.

Santiago chuckles before responding, and I almost twist my head to look at him.

"Brooklynn, I'm not disagreeing with you. You're right, and maybe I'm a little bit hurt by how much I agree with you. Really, you don't need to apologize." Santiago says, and I hear the smile in his voice.

"So you don't think that I'm this girl that's walking around telling you what your family should and shouldn't be doing?" I question, and this time I turn and meet his gaze, needing to see him reassure me.

"You're perfectly fine. I really mean it when I say that you didn't offend me with your comment. You don't need to walk on eggshells, you know?" Santiago says with a smile, squeezing my arm a little.

"Are you sure? I kind of still need you, so being a jerk really isn't something I should be doing."

"I'm glad my fake boyfriend services are enough to make sure you're not rude." Santiago says with a laugh, and I know that he's saying it as a joke and understands my full intentions, but for some reason, his words give me pause.

I didn't just mean that I needed him to be my fake boyfriend, but I also need him. He's more than just an actor in my elaborate plan. He's my friend, too.

"Santiago, where did you go last night? Why did you leave? Why are you bruised like this?" The words tumble out of my mouth as the silence echoes around us.

"There was a problem, and I had to fix it." Santiago takes a breath, and I feel the heaviness in it. "I did fix it."

CHAPTER 22

Santiago

"So, I think this boy is a little bit out of the scope of my abilities. Lynn, do you mind seeing what you can do with... this?" One of Brooklynn's makeup artists says after a few failed attempts at trying to cover the bruising on my face.

"Goodness, child, what did you even do?" Lynn—a middle-aged woman, probably around forty years old—asks as she stands in front of me, crossing her arms as she takes in her new canvas.

"Just...handling some stuff." I answer with a shrug, glancing over to see Brooklynn laughing with her artist as the woman applies something to her eyelashes, making her eyes look even larger than they already do.

"Yeah, well, can you handle stuff on days that aren't right before your girlfriend's movie premiere?" She teases, taking my face in her hand as she applies something cold to my face. I notice how she refers to me as Brooklynn's boyfriend, and I guess that Marie didn't tell anyone else about our little scheme.

"I'll try next time." I finally say, settling into the chair as she uses powders, creams, brushes, and sponges on my face.

When I met Brooklynn's parents on the plane ride over here, they'd both been a little bit wary of me, but over the course of the quick flight, they were both much more accepting and seemed to actually like me. Now, they're in their own trailer getting the finishing touches to their looks, while Brooklynn and I are in her designated trailer. Apparently, Marie didn't really pass on that information, either.

"All done, Mr. Santiago. What do you think?" Lynn asks thirty minutes later, and I survey myself in the mirror. Honestly, if I didn't know that most of my cheeks are bruised, I wouldn't be able to tell that there's any makeup on me.

"Wow, it's really good. Almost like they're not even here." I say with a smile, giving her a thumbs up.

"Almost?" She asks worriedly, her eyes scanning over my face as if to find a spot she missed.

"No, no, they're all covered, I was just referring to the fact that they're just a little bit sore, still."

"Oh, I'm sure. Now, I can't speak from experience—we girls tend to not show up to red carpets with blue and purple faces—but that looks extra nasty." Lynn says with a chuckle, dropping white cloves into my lap. "You're going to have to wear these because you'll be using your hands, and makeup will just smear after a while." She explains, her hands moving to place all of her products back into her makeup container.

I chuckle at her words, sliding the gloves on and standing to take a look at my appearance in the full-length mirror. Wow. While I usually wear tuxedos to all of The Enchanted Ivy parties, this one feels different.

"Hey, you don't look half bad, Santiago." Brooklynn teases as she moves to stand next to me. "I mean, we could do a little bit more cleaning up here, but it is what it is." She says, reaching up to brush her hand against the few stray hairs on my forehead. The gentle touch of her fingertips immediately causes me to swallow and take a few deep breaths. What is it about this that's making me so nervous?

"They're a part of the look, I think." I finally say, covering her hand with mine before fixing the hair. Brooklynn smiles at this and runs a hand over her own hair as if she must do *something* right now.

"Okay, then, Mr. Fashionable. The gloves are a nice touch, by the way, what's that about?"

"These are to cover the bruising." I reply nonchalantly, as though Brooklynn will take that for an answer.

"You're so frustrating." Brooklynn huffs. "Can you just tell me what happened? Pull me out of my misery?"

"Since I can tell you're not going to be satisfied until I tell you, I'll just say this: I had my suspicions about something, and the whole thing blew up that night." I say lightly, trying to brush off any more interest she might have. While I absolutely appreciate Brooklynn's concern, I don't want to be concerning *her* as she's preparing for literally one of the biggest nights of her life. Me being a complete fool isn't her fault, and making my worries her problem isn't right.

"What's that even supposed to mean?" Brooklynn says with a small laugh, sounding confused. "Wait, was this about Alessandro and Carmen? Did you find out about them dating?" She suddenly asks, her head snapping upward as though she's just realized this.

How in the world did she know about them? And why didn't she tell me?

"You knew about them?" My voice is lower than I'd like, but the depth behind my words is causing it. How and why did Brooklynn know about them before me, but also, why didn't she think to pass on that piece of information a little bit sooner, so I wouldn't look like the stupidest man alive when they kissed right in front of me?

"Yeah, about that..."

CHAPTER 23

Brooklynn

His reaction is one I should have expected when I blurted out that I knew his little sister and ex-friend were together. The words just came tumbling out, and I didn't think twice before I spoke. Stupid sleep-deprived brain for not thinking!

"So you mean to tell me that you knew since the school emergency that they're together?" Santiago says calmly. Too calmly, given the circumstances.

"Well, if I'm being completely honest, it was at least a week or two before that, because I saw them together all of the time and just assumed that they were a thing. Carmen kind of gave herself away that day, and then last night I saw them together, and that pretty much confirmed it." I take a pause, and then a theory flashes through my mind. "Hey, wait, don't tell me you beat up Alessandro," I state, suddenly realizing that I haven't seen Alessandro since then, too. "Oh my gosh, he's the person that you did this to," I say, brushing his hand, "and that did *this* to you." I finish, brushing his cheek lightly.

"Well, you're right about a lot of that, but he's not the person that did this," he taps his cheekbone, "or that caused these." Santiago says, pulling off his glove to show a few inches of his hands.

"Then who was it?" I breathe, all of the air suddenly leaving the room as Santiago's piercing gaze fixates on me. For some reason, whatever the conversation was just about, it doesn't matter anymore.

"Hey, it's time to get moving. Red carpet time, Brooklynn!" Marie calls out as she opens the door for a split second before closing it with a loud thud.

"We, um, we need to go." I quickly say, tearing my eyes away from Santiago and turning to the door. "Marie is going to give us another quick run-down, but then we're pretty much on our own after that, since she can't exactly give us instructions as we're in front of a billion cameras."

"Yes, of course." Santiago says from behind me as he follows, seemingly oblivious to the panic I'm feeling right now. Why in the world did it feel like all of the air had been removed from there? Why was Santiago looking at me like that? How did any of this-

"Brooklynn, it's time for you to get up there! Remember, deflect any and all Kai questions, and keep Santiago by your side at all times for a distraction." Marie says, gesturing towards the groups of actors, directors, and everyone else important for this movie, as they file in a line to the carpet.

"Here we go, Brooklynn. Your spotlight is waiting for you." Santiago says softly near my ear, the closeness causing the hairs on my neck to rise. I turn just in time to catch his face near mine, and a smile is dancing on his face as he straightens. How in the world did this amazing boy ever agree to take part in my crazy plans?

Walking down the carpet, I weave my fingers through Santiago as the bustle of everyone else covers my senses, the bright flashing lights ahead of us. Santiago doesn't say anything as I tighten my fingers in anticipation, rather he gives my hand a quick squeeze as the hoards of photographers and reporters buzz with excitement in anticipation of me. The rush that I'm feeling is exciting, but interestingly enough, I'm almost more excited for my hand to be intertwined with Santiago. The sparks of energy that crackle between us almost drown out the people around us, and as I step forward for our turn, it's like I've hit the end of a rope.

Turning, Santiago is smiling as he unclasps our hands, drawing his back to his side. "Brooklynn, you need to get all of the photos without me. This is about you, remember?" He teases, gesturing to the awaiting photographers and reporters.

"Oh yeah. Sorry, I just got carried away." For some reason, my voice is shy and quiet, a feeling I'm almost certain I've never felt before.

"Don't apologize. Go up there and have your moment." Santiago says easily, a genuine smile on his face as he gestures to the spot ahead of me.

Taking a few uncertain steps, I realize just how important Santiago was for this plan, and not only the fake boyfriend ways. With just the simple connection of having him by my side, any worry or nervousness was gone. Now, here I am, putting on my very best smile for everyone in the world, when the one person I want next to me waits on the sidelines.

My gaze wanders for the slightest of seconds, and that's when my breath catches in my throat. Kai is here, and talking to Santiago. Maintaining my dazzling smile, I quickly rush to Santiago and grip his arm, pulling him with me to the designated photo spot. There goes taking all of my photos myself. He's stunned for a split second, but immediately wraps his arm around my waist, and without looking, I know that he has his perfect smile out.

I'm not sure what possessed me to pull him up here, but for some reason, the notion took hold of me and I couldn't be more glad.

Someone on the sidelines motions that our turn is over, and we gracefully walk to the narrow passage that leads into the hotel, where the party and interviews will take place, hand in hand, the buzzing of people filling my ears.

"Hey, what happened to Brooklynn having her own spotlight?" Santiago whispers into my ear as we enter the dazzling ballroom filled with celebrities and photographers. My eyes never turn to face him, the stunning gold lights and shimmering dresses almost blinding me in the best way possible.

"I don't know." Is my honest answer as I do a small twirl and survey the room. "My parents should be in here any minute now." I'm not sure where the words come from, but I'm ecstatic to see them and ask what they thought of me on the carpet that they've been walking together for years.

"I'll keep an eye out for them." Santiago says softly, his hand tightening around mine. I squeeze his hand lightly before turning my attention back to the excitement around me. Everything is painted in the illumination of excitement and of something *new* and *big*.

"You both were amazing out there. Although I'm not sure why you pulled Santiago up there. Whatever, though. Regardless, I haven't seen anything about you and Kai on the internet; rather, it's about you two." Marie gushes as we all head into our hotel rooms, her chattering voice both reassuring and irritating. The reason for the irritation is only because the waves of tiredness that are crashing over me every minute that I'm not asleep.

Apparently, the more tired I get, the more irritable I get. Which is a completely new feeling for me, because I guess I've never been this tired before. After standing and talking with more people than I'll ever remember, the car ride through traffic, and the twenty stories that we had to walk up because the elevator was closed for the night—apparently that's a thing, criminal if you ask me—and Marie energized and ready to critique everything I did and didn't do, I'm kind of done.

"Marie, I think Brooklynn is a tiny bit overwhelmed." Santiago says lightly, his tone almost teasing as he speaks, but I can hear the depth in his voice as he gently takes one for the team and lets Marie down easily.

"Oh, well, of course, but still-"

"Look, here's our room. Brooklynn, you're beside us, Santiago, you're across, and Marie, I think you're a few rooms down?" Mom interjects, her expression kind, but I've been her daughter long enough to know when she's hanging on by a thread, and while we're not exactly to that point just yet, it's coming. "Everyone's luggage should be in your rooms, but if not, we can work something out." With that, she uses the card to her room and slips inside with Dad following, the door clicking shut behind them. Marie walks a few doors down to her room and does the same, leaving Santiago and me in the hallway.

"Good night, Santiago. You were really amazing tonight. Thank you." I say, looking up as I talk, Santiago's eyes fixed on me. He doesn't make a move to reply for a minute, and for the silliest of moments, I wonder if I even spoke.

"I did nothing. You were shining without me, really." Santiago answers modestly. His refusal to accept a compliment only irritates me slightly, because I know why he's doing it. Still, I would enjoy it if he would recognize that I really appreciate him.

"Well, it appears that you're never going to accept my compliment, so we'll just leave it at that. Have a nice night." I say with a smile, turning for my door, only to be stopped as Santiago's hand grasps my wrist. Turning, my curious gaze meets his somewhat serious one. "Do you have something to say, Mr. Alvarez?" I tease, the warmth from his hand sending my train of thought slightly out of sorts.

"It's not that I won't accept a compliment, but you were seriously okay without me. You would have been amazing on your own, and you should see that before you rush to compliment me." Santiago explains, his voice swirling around the hallway. Once his words settle in my brain, along with the touch from his hand, the need to retreat into my room overwhelms me.

"Thanks, Santiago. I'll see you tomorrow." I rush out, slipping my wrist away, scurrying into my room. Only when the door is latched behind me do I allow myself to take a breath, the strangest feeling rushing through my body. Whatever it is, I try to push it aside as I take a quick shower and dress for bed, but the feeling persists. Even after I've finally crawled into bed, my thoughts are still a mess, and I'm thankful for sleep.

CHAPTER 24
Brooklynn

"So, are you going to tell me why you're all bruised?" I ask Santiago, the question nagging at me. We have another hour before we need to be ready for makeup and outfits, so we're currently lounging in his suite on the couches, homework spread around us. Mom and Dad went out to lunch, but advised that we stay here, just in case the paparazzi finds them.

"Do you really want to know?" Santiago questions, looking up from the paper he's reading.

"I don't know, maybe I should ask you another twenty times, just for good measure." I say flatly, meeting his gaze as I speak.

"Fair enough." Santiago says with a sigh, dropping the paper on his neat stack of assignments. "I saw Carmen walk down a hallway, and didn't think anything of it until that guy, Emilio, followed her."

"Oh no." Is my only response. I see where this is going.

"And when I caught up to them, he was trying to get his

hands on her, and pretty much after that, Alessandro and I handled him." Santiago states. "We all went home right after that, since I wasn't really able to drive, and that's pretty much it. Oh, also, that's when I found out they were together, because Carmen kissed Alessandro right in front of me."

"That's...quite the story." I finally say. "You're a great brother to Carmen."

"Thanks, I guess. It's all kind of a blur, and I just want to move past it." Santiago says with a small laugh.

"So are you angry that they're dating?" I can't help myself from asking, because if he's going to be answering my questions, I might as well get them all out now.

"Honestly, it shocked me, but I can't really do anything, and if they really like each other, then I shouldn't." Santiago answers, pressing his lips together before continuing. "And I know that Alessandro is a good guy at heart, so I'm not worried about him hurting her."

"You're so mature about all of this. I'm sorry for dragging you all of the way to New York just hours after you went through all of that." I apologize, feeling more than a little bit bad about the timing of everything.

"Don't worry about it. This is actually probably better than having to go back to normal the next day." Santiago says reassuringly, his eyes staring deeply into mine as he speaks.

"Thank you." Is all I can get out. Something about right now feels strange, almost as though my words aren't working properly. However, it doesn't necessarily feel wrong.

"You're looking dazzling, Brooklynn. This is the *perfect* color for you." Lynn says after stepping back to admire the hair, makeup, and dress that I've been done up in. After doing a quick twirl in the mirror, I have to agree that everything is fits me perfectly.

My curls have been diffused and filled with product to keep their naturally tighter pattern, and my makeup has been placed in all of the right places, accentuating my natural features. The dress that was chosen for me is an old mauve tone, and I can't believe how nicely it fits me, but also how well the color looks on me. The stylist in charge of this whole look really thought everything through, and I don't have a single complaint.

"Thank you, Lynn. I think you did an amazing job with me." I say with a smile, brushing the sides of my dress as I wait for Santiago to come out from behind the curtain, where Susan is doing the finishing touches on his face.

"Hey, Brooklynn, I just added a little bit of glitter and hairspray. My canvas was already stunning." Lynn replies, placing her hand on her hip like she actually wants me to listen. "You shouldn't be telling yourself that, you know."

"Thank you, but you-"

"None of that, now. I know what you're going to say, and it's going to contradict what I've already said." Lynn interrupts with a *hush* hand movement.

There's no chance for me to reply, because just then, Santiago emerges from his side of the room, and my breath is actually taken away. There's not much difference in his tuxedo from last night, but for some reason, seeing him is creating this reaction within me that I'm not sure I can decipher.

Santiago's hair is combed in all of the right places, but still slightly messy here and there. With his tuxedo and gloves, he really fits the fake-boyfriend bill. He almost fits the bill a little bit *too* well.

"You look...very pretty, Brooklynn." Santiago says, his eyes taking in my whole dress and hair, his expression one that I'm not sure I've ever seen him wear.

"Thank you, Santiago," I say with a smile, noticing a little bit too late how soft my voice sounds. Maybe not *soft*, but there's definitely something unusual about it. Something I can't quite place my finger on just yet. "You look passable, yourself." I tease, needing to break whatever strange tone is in my voice.

"Thank you, I guess?" Santiago jokes back, the expression on his face disappearing as quickly as it appeared.

"Yeah, take it as a compliment, but don't let it make its way to your head *too* much. We wouldn't want you floating away, now would we?" My smile is one of amusement, and Santiago's face mirrors it for a moment. The way his full smile is appearing only now, and how there are a few lines at the edge of his eyes, are suddenly the most fascinating things in the world. His eyes settle on mine, and instead of shifting my focus like my brain says to do, they only gaze even deeper into the brown depths of his eyes. Something about them is so entrancing, and for a moment, it feels as though the emotion behind them is telling me something that I can't quite understand.

"Are we ready, you two?" A shrill voice calls out,

bringing me back to earth as I realize where I am. Santiago's eyes shift, and the view of my perfect fake boyfriend is gone.

"Yes, we are. On our way." Santiago says coolly, as though there wasn't just enough tension in the air to power a city. Well, maybe not a *city*, but definitely most of one. Santiago extends his arm to me, and for the slightest of seconds, I hesitate to wrap my hand through it. What if something like whatever just happened, happens at the premiere later? "Brooklynn?"

"Yes, let's go." I quickly respond, slipping my hand into the crook of Santiago's elbow and allowing him to lead me to the door. Well, whatever just happened won't be happening later, and if I even start to slightly feel like I'm slipping into some sort of Santiago-induced trance, then I'll stop it.

Once we've arrived at the hotel where the premiere will be held, Marie steps out and opens our door, with Santiago exiting first, then extending his hand for me. Mustering up enough courage for the rest of the night, I slip out of the car, smiling brightly as we walk the red carpet into the grand hotel. More cameras are waiting inside, and as we reach the base of the grand staircase, I quickly glance back at the photographers and wonder how I'll manage this without flashing them. Santiago follows my eyes, and immediately, his expression changes. Wordlessly, he slips off his tuxedo jacket and stands behind me, using it as an extra barrier between my legs and the cameras.

"They won't be able to see anything, now." Santiago says quietly. Something about his voice is more protective and mature than how he usually speaks, and I can't help but turn my gaze to his face. For a moment, I'm awestruck. In my peripheral vision, I can see the flashing of a million cameras, but it's as though they're a world away. Santiago's face is maybe more beautiful than I've ever seen, and for the life of me, I don't know why. "Brooklynn?" His voice brings me back to reality, and I quickly turn and walk up the stairs, having already done what I promised myself I wouldn't do.

Marie and my parents are waiting in the hallway, and after giving me a once-over, Marie motions to the usher, who leads Santiago and me to our seats in the very front row, which, ever so conveniently, places me in between Kai and Santiago.Reminding myself of all of the media training I've received, I give Kai a polite smile as I sit, still closely gripping Santiago's arm. The one interesting thing I notice is that Rachel isn't on Kai's arm, which is rather strange, since they're together, right? Or did he make that up?

"We have the perfect view, Santiago," I comment, needing to say something and remind myself that I have full control over this situation.

"I get to see all of your acting up close." Santiago says, his tone professional, but I hint of his teasing one slightly audible.

"Yeah-"

"I'm sure you'll be impressed with our chemistry. The directors couldn't believe how real it was." Kai says, opening his mouth and interrupting me. Oh great, he's going to be doing this. I'm about to reply coolly, but before I can even form words, Santiago is speaking.

"I can definitely believe it. Brooklynn is an amazing actress, and she never fails to impress me with how real her emotions look on screen. I always have to remind myself that they're on screen, and not real." Wow, Santiago completely stood up for me *and* shut down Kai, all while staying professional and complimenting me. Inwardly, I smile, but outwardly, I keep my expression calm and composed, not even hinting at the fact that Santiago just made my whole evening.

"I have to agree. We're both such amazing actors. It's no wonder our other movie did so well." Kai says after a few moments, obviously needing to patch up his ego after neither of us took his bait. Santiago seemingly deliberates before responding, and I'm curious as to what he's going to reply with.

"Brooklynn was wonderful there. I almost don't remember any of the plot or other characters in it, if I'm being honest. My eyes were glued to her the entire time." Santiago continues, obviously hearing Kai trying to stroke his own ego.

"You're laying it on thick," I whisper to Santiago, quiet enough that there's surely no way Kai heard me, but close enough to Santiago's ear that my voice is audible.

"And?" Santiago questions with a smirk, wrapping his arm around my shoulder before leaning close, as though he's trying to whisper, but his next words are clearly meant for more ears than just mine. "I just love showing off my amazing girlfriend." A blush flushes my cheeks, and I find myself burying my face softly into his arm to conceal the pink that's flooding my skin. Immediately, Santiago's scent washes over me, and for an instant, I completely lose focus of where I am and what I'm doing. What am I even thinking? No. This is a *public* premiere, and I need to be acting *professionally*.

The opening credits start rolling, and I begrudgingly

settle into my chair, allowing the voice—my voice—to open the first scene in the movie. Instead of watching the movie like a normal person, I try to remember each of the scenes as they were recorded. With all of the microphones, cameras, scripts, directors, and Kai. A feeling of sickness washes over me as I remember thinking that we were friends. Little did I know, just barely a year later, he would be purposely tearing down my reputation.

"Hey, are you okay?" Santiago asks gently, his breath tickling my ear and neck, the sensation strange in the state of emotion that I'm currently in.

"Yeah, of course." I quickly whisper back, forcing the fakest of smiles for him. Santiago frowns for a moment before gently brushing the tips of his fingers against my smile, allowing my lips to drop to a resting position.

"Brooklynn, you don't have to be okay. I'm here for you." Santiago's words are even quieter than before, and I'm grateful for his discretion.

"I'll tell you about it later." I finally say, giving him a promising look before turning back to the movie. The first kiss is about to happen, and out of my peripheral vision, Kai has turned to watch me as I continue to watch the movie emotionlessly. His character is leaning in, and on-screen Brooklynn wraps her arms around his neck and pulls him closer as they kiss, the rain pouring down around them. Kai keeps his eyes on me, and I can't tell if it's because he's trying to get my reaction to the movie, or if he's interested in my little conversation with Santiago. Either way, I refuse to give him any type of acknowledgment, and stare on at the screen. Goodness. How long is this kiss scene?

CHAPTER 25

Santiago

I can't help but let my eyes wander back to Brooklynn's straight posture and rigid jawline. Something about watching her struggle while viewing the movie moves something within me. Kai seems to be doing the same thing I'm doing, and I want to demand that he remove his gaze from her. He has no right to watch her so intently when he has nothing but bad intentions for her.

As the movie nears what must be the last quarter, the curiosity over what Brooklynn is going to tell me later nags at me, but true to Brooklynn's wishes, I don't bring it up again. A little bit of patience wouldn't hurt me.

"Are you sure this is allowed?" This is probably my third time repeating those words, but truthfully, I just don't want Brooklynn to get in trouble.

"If you ask me that again, I might call security on you just for the fun of it. Then, they will tell you that this is perfectly acceptable." Brooklynn teases, knocking her shoulder into mine as she splashes her feet in the hot tub.

"Whatever you say, Miss Movie Star." I tease, watching her eyes as I speak.

"Hey, let's not bring any of my *many* titles into this argument," Brooklynn says with a swish of her curls, a smile on her lips. A few more minutes pass by before either of us speaks, the windy rooftop filling in the gaps of our silence. We're the only people up here—probably due to the fact that it's somewhere around three in the morning—and the sound of the jets sending water bubbles into our feet is comforting.

"What were you going to tell me earlier?" I finally ask, and Brooklynn's foot stops swishing the water for a split second.

"I was just thinking about how much I used to enjoy Kai's company, and now he's trying to destroy me." She pauses before continuing, her tone careful. "I was so new and naive, and I feel like I should have seen this coming."

"Yeah, I get why you feel like that, but there was no way for you to know." I sympathize.

"No, you don't know. I don't see Mr. Movie Star in your list of titles." Brooklynn teases, and before I can try to explain, she's pushing me into the hot tub, her surprise attack catching me completely off-guard.

"Hey, what was that about?" I yelp, the warm water instantly removing the night chill from my body.

"I'm not sure, actually. I've been thinking about pushing

you in for at least thirty minutes, and I couldn't hold back any longer." She admits, and my jaw drops.

"So your attack was premeditated? Wow." I joke, trying to sound horrified. "You know, that could really get you in trouble." I say, wrapping my arms around Brooklynn's torso and pulling her in with me, catching *her* completely off guard.

CHAPTER 26

Brooklynn

Santiago's arms are the first thing that my brain registers, the next being how well-defined and muscled his chest is. Both of those thoughts surprise me, but not because I wasn't expecting them, more so because I'm truly notching them. He's still wrapped around my waist, and our bodies are pressed together, much closer than they've ever been. I risk glancing up at him for some indication of what he's doing, but his face is completely still. His lips are slightly parted, and it almost seems as though Santiago's eyes are softer than they've ever been.

Lowering my eyes, I watch as the water droplets run down his neck and into the wet shirt that he's wearing. It's plastered to Santiago's body, and my eyes shift to his arms. Still, they're wrapped around my waist, completely unwavering and still. My leggings and tank top are now soaked, but due to the hot tub, I'm not cold. Or, maybe it's the heat radiating off of Santiago. At this point, I'm not really sure.

Again, I raise my eyes to Santiago's, but this time, I don't look away. Maybe it's all of the hours I've been awake catching up to me, or maybe it's the seemingly increasing temperature of the hot tub, but Santiago feels closer. His body closer to mine, his arms tighter around my waist, his face a mere few inches away. Looking up through my eyelashes, Santiago is staring just as intently into my eyes as I am at him.

I'm not sure what comes over me, but I reach up and wrap my arms around his neck, pulling him impossibly closer. And then, one moment my eyes are wide open, and there's space between us, and the next, Santiago's lips are on mine, and there's a flurry of lights behind my closed eyes.

For just a moment, I'm completely still, but some part of me takes over, and suddenly, I'm kissing Santiago back. Instead of questioning if I should even be doing this, I focus on the present. My lips move against his as I allow my hands to gather strands of his hair and weave them around my fingers, my nails gently scraping against the back of his neck as I do so. Everywhere that we're touching feels electrically charged, and if I opened my eyes, I wouldn't be surprised to see actual lightning bolts in the air around us.

Santiago's arms tighten around my waist, and one of his hands slips up my side, leaving the places his hand brushed tingling and electrified, with his hand ending up on my cheek, cupping my face as he kisses me back. His thumb brushes my cheek before twirling a few of my curls around his finger, which he keeps there for a few seconds before tucking the strands behind my ear. For some reason, his careful actions with my hair makes me smile against his lips, and it reminds me that I'm probably being the exact opposite of careful with his hair right now. I loosen my grip on his hair, suddenly embarrassed by how out of control I'm being.

"Don't stop." Santiago breathes, and for a moment, I'm not sure what he's talking about. "Keep doing that to my hair. It feels nice." He elaborates. Giggling against his lips, I return my fingers to the base of his neck, intertwining his hair once more with my fingers. Only, this time, I pay attention to the reaction his skin has to my touch. Goosebumps flood his skin against my fingertips, and knowing that *I'm* causing this reaction sends a rush throughout my body, and some sort of emotional response in my head.

"Hey, is someone up here?" A loud, male voice calls through the darkness. My eyes jerk open, and it's as though I've been shocked—not in a good way—because in one instant, I'm nowhere near Santiago, and I'm completely out of the hot tub.

"Yes, we are." Santiago calls out breathlessly, quickly climbing out, too. I nervously look around for a towel, but remembering that coming up to the pool wasn't originally in my agenda for four in the morning, that means I'm towel-less, cold, and quite frankly, scared. Who is even up here right now?

"Who's we?" The man finally emerges from the darkness, and he seems to be some sort of hotel employee. "I'm the upper-level security and was doing my rounds. Sorry for disrupting your morning." He says as he takes us in, surely concluding that we weren't playing mermaids in the hot tub, all alone, at four in the morning.

"No problem, sir. Sorry for any inconvenience to you, as well." Santiago says calmly and politely.

"No inconvenience at all, have a nice morning," The man says, quickly turning and exiting through the door that will lead him to the staircase. I feel Santiago turn to me, and before he can even speak, I start talking.

"We should be getting back, since we have to get up in a few hours." I quickly say, walking to the exit, Santiago close behind me as I do so.

"Maybe we can ta-"

"I'm actually really tired, can we just go right back to our rooms?" Rude of me to interrupt, I know, but if I let this go any farther, I might just have a mental breakdown in the middle of a hotel stairwell. Santiago doesn't try to speak again, and I'm glad. As we reach our hallway, I quickly swipe my keycard and enter my room, carefully locking my door before collapsing on the bed.

What have I done?

I kissed Santiago.

I *kissed* Santiago.

I kissed *Santiago.*

What's wrong with me? This was never a part of the plan. How did I get so wrapped up in tonight that I *kissed* him? How am I supposed to come back from that, now? I can't just kiss someone and then expect to forget it all the next day. What am I even supposed to do now? Deep down, my emotions are still swirling, and the desire to kiss him again is strong. *So* strong.

Do I even like Santiago like that? Is this just some concoction of emotions that's come to life due to the romance movie, and Santiago being the best fake boyfriend ever created? Surely I don't actually want Santiago like that, right?

After hours of interviews, cameras, and reporters, we're finally on the plane back home. *Home.* Just a few weeks ago, I'm not sure I would have called it that, but after being in school, being in The Enchanted Ivy, and Santiago, home is actually beginning to feel like home.

At just the thought of Santiago's name, my eyes travel over to the seat he's occupying a few feet away. His leather jacket is folded neatly across his lap, and while I can't be sure, since he's wearing sunglasses, he appears to be sleeping. I don't blame him, though. Today has been draining, and after last night, I don't think I'll be resting anytime soon. We still haven't talked about what happened, and to be honest, I'm not sure how to bring it up. Of course, we haven't had time today, but Santiago has acted as though nothing happened, and I'm not sure if that's a good or bad thing. Does it mean nothing to him, and he just let loose after being awake for countless hours, and a steamy hot tub kiss was the way to do that? Is he waiting for a calmer moment to bring it up because it *did* mean something to him?

If I could go back in time, I probably wouldn't have allowed myself to kiss him, because look at where we are now. I'm confused, and we've possibly just ruined whatever our relationship is.

Did I enjoy kissing him last night? Absolutely. Does

knowing he's an amazing kisser he is make me want to kiss him again? The answer is one hundred and ten percent yes.

The thing is, I'm not sure if I've ever fully looked at Santiago that way. I don't want to be kissing him like that if he's not my boyfriend, but I haven't ever looked at him in a way that made me consider him as my actual boyfriend. Somehow, I got so wrapped up in this whole fake-boyfriend scheme and failed to realize that Santiago was right in front of my face. Another factor is that I have to consider Santiago may not like me like that.

Who's to say that he wants to date me for real? I don't want to be pining after him if he has no interest in me. There's no more time for me to overthink my Santiago situation since we're landing, but the entire drive back to my house, and up until the very last moment before my brain stops working before I fall asleep, I think of him.

CHAPTER 27

Santiago

"Santiago, do you have any idea of what level of publicity this has brought to your siblings and us? You didn't even think to tell us twelve hours before you hopped on a plane to New York with a movie star, a mere few hours after you got in that fight?" Mother asks from across Father's large office desk, her cup of tea sitting right next to a stack of neatly piled papers. Father watches me intently from next to Mother, as he waits for my response.

"Was the publicity bad? I told you as soon as I got confirmation on when we would be leaving. Would you have preferred for that disgusting man to be attacking Carmen?" I say these lines without a hint of sarcasm, the questions genuine, even though I'm sure I already know the answers.

"Well, I mean, the publicity *is* good, especially for your sister. As long as nothing bad comes of it, your relationship with that actress is fine. And, you are right about that terrible man. Thank you, Santiago." Wait, did Father just agree with me, say that I was right, and then *compliment* me all in one breath? Am I dreaming right now? There is no way that in this reality all of those things just happened.

"Your Father is right. We don't want anything negative to come publicity-wise from your relationship, but other than that, we don't have any complaints." Okay, someone is about to splash me with ice water to wake me up, because this is seriously insane. "But on the other hand, we're still dealing with your sister and her...relationship." Mother says, eyeing me as though I knew something about this before that night, a few days ago. As if. There wasn't a single bone in my body that saw Alessandro and Carmen getting together.

"Did you know anything about that, Santiago?" Father finally questions, watching me intently as if he'll be able to tell if I lie.

"I didn't. Trust me."

"Okay, then. We're about to be on our way to a little party that Renee is throwing, but we're happy to see you back here." Mother says, waving her hand in a dismissive gesture. I take this as my cue to leave, and just before I reach my room a few minutes later, Carmen pops out of her room and into the hallway.

"Santiago! What in the world? Why did you hide the fact that you were dating *my* friend, and that you were going to be flying off to New York City, and that you were going to be famous?" Carmen demands, grabbing my arm as though that could actually stop me. Of course, if I wanted to keep moving, I easily could, but there's no point in dragging her behind me as I make a desperate attempt to escape to my room.

"That's quite the statement coming from you." I quip, meeting her gaze as I speak.

"What do you mean?" Carmen has the audacity to look confused, and I restrain myself from laughing in her face.

"You're dating my *ex-best* friend, Carmen." I say carefully, watching her reaction.

"Oh, about that." She sucks in a few breaths before talking again. "Look, I didn't get to explain everything because you left that morning, but I promise I will." Carmen rushes.

"No-" I begin.

"Yes, Santiago. It was maybe a little bit insensitive to do that, but you don't know the full story, and-"

"Carmen, you don't owe me the full story. If you're happy with him, then I just want to be left out of it."

"Santiago, did you hit your head or something?" Carmen suddenly asks, reaching up and grabbing my face to inspect my eyes.

"No, why?" I ask, shaking my face to loosen her grip.

"You just don't really sound like yourself." Yeah, try kissing the girl who doesn't like you, and have her run off and not even act like anything happened. That really does something to your brain.

"I need to go to sleep. I've had a long day, and I just need rest." I finally say, stepping into my room and closing the door before she can protest.

It's not that I'm upset with Carmen, but I don't feel like having this conversation with her right now. Especially with the headspace I'm in with Brooklynn. Just the thought of her name feels like a ray of sunshine on my body, her name immediately bringing the feeling of warmth and softness.

Why did she run off and avoid me after we kissed? I thought I completely read her signals right. She was kissing me back, and not showing any signs of being uncomfortable like I was too handsy or something. Was it something I did after?

There has never been another girl that I've been this confused about. Maybe it's because Brooklynn is hard to read, but I know deep down that it's because she's the first girl I've really ever cared about. Sure, I've liked other girls, but nothing like this. Brooklynn is the only girl I've ever cared about this much. It's scary how much I like her.

Admitting all of this to myself tightens my throat as I toss and turn in my bed, and I almost consider finding my keys and going out for a midnight drive to clear my head. *Almost.* I'm still smart enough to know that I'm too tired for that, and it wouldn't be fun to have my car wrapped around a tree a mile down the road.

I need to talk to Brooklynn soon. It's not fair to leave her feeling awkward about our kiss when, technically, I was the one to initiate it. Even if she kissed me back, I am still responsible for the aftermath. I'm not sure if she is feeling awkward, but it wouldn't be a stretch to assume so, right?

Carmen was pretty quiet on the way to school, but I don't blame her. I was more than a little bit rude last night, and the last time she saw me before that was when I beat that creep off of her, and found out she's dating my ex-best friend. That can't be a super comfortable position to be in, I'm sure.

Striding through the halls, I find a swarm of students around someone, and it takes me less than a second to recognize the voice that's being surrounded. Brooklynn.

"Hey, there's the lucky guy who's spending the weekend in New York with Brooklynn." A loud, male voice calls out, his tone more than suggestive—and suspicious—as he speaks. A chorus of agreements comes from the group, and I grumble before pushing through them and into the center of the circle that's around Brooklynn's locker.

"It's time for everybody to get moving. Leave Brooklynn alone." The words come out firmly, and the protectiveness in my voice is unmistakable. My message is clear, and most of the people get on with their lives. However, a group of four boys from my class hang around, clearly not going to let up.

"Says who? Brooklynn, do you want us to leave?" One of them says defensively. For the first time, I meet her eyes as she glances around somewhat nervously.

"Well, it would be nice not to be followed around," Brooklynn starts, clearly not wanting to ruffle as many feathers as possible. Which is understandable. However, she should be able to tell a group of rude boys to leave her alone without that worry. "I have to get to class, have a nice day." Brooklynn hastily says, pushing past the group and walking in the direction of her class.

The Enchanted Ivy is hosting a party for one of the members, an ultra-rich businessman that Father is friends with. So, of course, it needs to be a whole event with all of the club members invited.

Carmen and Matteo are in front of me as we walk through the large doors, and I immediately spot Alessandro waiting for Carmen. Gritting my teeth, I continue walking. I know that I need to talk to Alessandro soon, but the thought still places a bitter taste in my mouth. The taste immediately evaporates as I spot Brooklynn across the room, her black dress fitting her to perfection.

My eyes take in every small detail of her. From every curl, to her smile, to the gold rings that adorn her fingers, I take it all in. As if she senses my staring, Brooklynn turns to me, her eyes immediately changing. Taking this as my cue to approach her, I start in her direction, the woman she's talking to—Daniela—notices and touches Brooklynn's arm before striding off.

"You look beautiful." The words spill out of my mouth before I can even decide if that's how I want to greet her, but Brooklynn's cheeks turn slightly pink at this, so it must be the right thing. I don't know where all of my confidence with women has gone since meeting Brooklynn, but here I am, questioning all of my words and actions like I've been known to say the wrong things or something.

"Thank you, Santiago. You look very dashing, yourself." Brooklynn responds, quickly looking me up and down before averting her gaze to the man that the party is for. The staff is wheeling out the ginormous cake, and other partygoers are starting to move in that direction. I don't care about what's going on over there, but Brooklynn's expression is blank as she watches the scene unfolding.

"So, how was school this morning?" I question, unsure of what to say, because usually, Brooklynn starts our conversations.

"It was fine, thank you." She says, barely meeting my eyes before shifting her gaze to the golf course that's bathed in the golden sunset, the floor-to-ceiling windows giving the perfect view of the scene.

"Did they leave you alone after that?" I try again, unsure of what I'm doing wrong.

"Yes, they did," Brooklynn says. She seems to consider something before completely turning and starting to walk away from me. What?

"Hey, are you okay?" I ask after taking a few long strides, falling into step next to her. Her expression is almost unreadable, but there's a touch of hurt in her eyes that I can't quite figure out.

"Yeah, of course," Brooklynn responds, her voice clipped and formal.

"Yeah, I'm sure." I say, my voice coming out frustrated and slightly rude.

"What's that supposed to mean?" She demands, turning and standing in front of me. Brooklynn's curls bounce as she does so, and the overwhelming desire to reach out and run my hands through them suddenly takes over my body, but using all of the self-control I have, I refrain from doing so.

"It means that you're obviously not okay, but for some reason, you feel like you need to lie to me."

"It's very bold of you to assume something about me, Mr. Alvarez," Brooklynn says sharply, her eyes narrowed.

"It's very bold of you to assume that I don't know when

you're lying. Miss Carmine." My words come out slightly sharp, even though that wasn't fully my intention.

"Santiago, please just leave me alone. I need some space right now, and I don't want to be causing a scene at some ancient billionaire's birthday party." Brooklynn finally responds after staring directly into my eyes for a few seconds, as though she's searching them for something. This really isn't how I planned this interaction going when I approached her earlier.

"What are you saying, Brooklynn? What's wrong?" My voice is softer now as her words really sink in. Laughter floats from behind us as the partygoers celebrate, but it's all background noise as I focus on Brooklynn.

"I'm saying that I need a break from..." She trails off as she softens her gaze. "*This*." She moves her hand between us as though that explains what she's talking about.

"What do you mean? What's *this*?" I question, frustration at the edges of my voice.

"You're right, Santiago. What is *this*?" Brooklynn says somewhat sharply, again, gesturing between us, and something clicks. She's done with me. She got what she needed for a fake boyfriend, and now she's done with me.

"You tell me. You're the one who came up with this little ruse that painted me as your perfect boyfriend." The words are sharper now, but the sharpness is blanketing my hurt. How was I so foolish to think that I meant anything to Brooklynn?

"Oh, so this is all on me now? Okay then. Goodbye, Santiago. Our little *ruse* is over. Thank you for everything." She snaps.

"*Use* is more like it." I say under my breath, but Brooklynn doesn't catch it, as she's already spun on her heels and is gracefully walking out of the room.

And just like that, she's done with me.

CHAPTER 28
Brooklynn

Sucking in a deep breath, I walk through the large doors and into the cool night, needing to find fresh air after my conversation with Santiago. How did that all just go so south? How did I allow all of this to happen? How did I allow myself to believe that there was maybe something between us?

The night air chills my exposed arms, and goosebumps flood my arms and shoulders as I walk one of the paths, presumably leading to the gardens. Maybe this was never meant to happen, and Santiago was never meant to be part of my life. But maybe he was supposed to stick around much longer than just a few short weeks while he helped me out. Maybe he was supposed to be my person as I settled into life here.

The soft billowing of the plants and flowers in the breeze is comforting as I stride through the garden path, remembering how Santiago and I strode through them all of those weeks ago.

I've really gone and messed things up with him, haven't I? Why did I ever allow him to kiss me and mess with my head like that? We were going to go back to being friends, but now that we've kissed, how is that even possible? I know what his lips taste like, and how his hair is unbelievably soft when my fingers run through it. I can't just forget those things and act like nothing happened. I could have pretended like the Santiago effect wasn't strong, and that I was completely okay with being friends, but after that, I don't even see friends as a possibility now.

"Brooklynn?" A voice calls out from behind me, and a scream escapes my lips. "Hey, it's just me, Daniela." Her voice is recognizable now, but that still doesn't calm down my racing heart.

"Why did you sneak up on me like that? I think you gave me a heart attack." I gasp out, stopping so she can catch up to me.

"Sorry, sorry. I just saw you leave in a rush and wanted to check on you, and maybe escape that stuffy party for a few minutes." Daniela apologizes, sounding sincere. I find humor in it, though, and can't help but tease her.

"I see, you just needed an excuse to leave, and felt like scaring me in the process," I say with a smirk, and Daniela's lips lift in a smile.

"Here I was trying to check on you, and now I'm the victim." She teases. "But, regardless of how easily you just flipped the tables, are you okay?" Daniela's voice is softer now, and I watch her carefully, as though that's going to give me the answer on whether or not to tell her what's happening. I decide on the partial truth, and sit down on one of the garden benches as I suck in a breath.

"Well, Santiago and I are kind of fighting right now." Is all I say, waiting for her reaction before continuing.

"That's understandable. You're both probably really stressed after being in New York and dealing with all of the movie stuff. Right?" She has a point that would make sense if we were actually dating, but that's the fun part about fake dating: you can't exactly get any advice, because you're already lying about most of the situation.

"I guess you could say that." I hum. It *is* true that New York added a whole new layer to our relationship, but not in the way that she thinks. "We've just been having problems, and I think I really hurt his feelings back there, and I'm not sure how to fix things." The answer is truthful, because my saying that we're done is kind of something that most people would take more than a little bit of offense to.

"Well, I don't know exactly what to tell you, but I think you need to figure out what and who is and isn't important to you, and focus on the things that are grouped in the important category. You're a smart and kind girl, as long as you're honest with yourself, you'll work this out." Daniela pats my arm before turning back to the party. "If you want something or *someone*, then you need to act on it." And with that, she's leaving me by myself.

She made a bunch of fair points, but she also doesn't know the full extent of what went down. At this point, I promise myself to just go home and sleep on all of the mistakes I've made. Tears are beginning to roll down my cheeks as I walk to our car, sliding into the backseat and instructing our driver to take me home. Mom and Dad won't be coming home for at least another hour, so there will be plenty of time for Mr. Stone to get back to them before they need to be driven home.

Awakening to the gentle morning sunlight streaming through my windows almost makes me forget everything that went down last night. The keyword being *almost*. Well, last night's bad decisions—as well as the hot tub incident— are going to be fun to think about when I undoubtedly see Santiago at school later. There's something about him that, no matter where we are, I'm able to find him without trying. That will surely be the case today.

Within five minutes of being on school grounds, I've already seen Santiago, and sickeningly enough, with a female entourage. Even though it looks like he's not paying them any attention, just seeing a group of them around him when we're technically still together—by the media's standards, at least—it still rubs me completely the wrong way. Whatever, though. It's not like I'm going to do anything about it. Even though the world is still under the assumption that we're together, it's not like anything about us not being together will get out anytime soon. We were never really affectionate or anything at school, and no one at The Enchanted Ivy will even bat an eyelash, because we're pretty irrelevant to them. Still, girls following him around when he was *just* on the red carpet with me is annoying.

Soon enough, though, I have my own male entourage following me, and it takes all of my willpower not to turn and just tell them to leave. If I do that, then I'm going to be frustrated, and with how frustrated I already am, that will probably be the straw that breaks the camel's back.

Paying them no mind, I continue on to my locker, quickly opening it and grabbing one of my books before turning and heading to my classroom, the group of boys still a few feet behind me, as though they think I'm not aware that they're following me.

As I reach my class, they all go their separate ways, since they're all most likely a grade ahead of me. I spot Carmen a few seats ahead of me, and for a moment, I consider trying to talk to her. Which is weird, because we haven't talked all that much since I got back here. I wonder if she's upset with me since I'm "dating" her brother, and took him on a red carpet for the world to see, without even mentioning it to her. It's not like we were extremely close or anything, but we did hang out a few times. Maybe within the next few days I'll try talking to her again, but I'm not sure how that will go, since apparently Santiago and I are over, and that will just be awkward.

CHAPTER 29
Santiago

Something about seeing a group of my classmates following Brooklynn around like a pack of wolves stirs deep rage within me, but Brooklynn doesn't even seem to care. Something about that enrages me even more. Maybe she's already tried to tell them to leave, and they haven't, but judging by her emotionless expression, she hasn't even tried anything, and that makes me even more upset. Just as I'm considering saying something, Carmen walks over to me, Alessandro in tow. He doesn't look uncomfortable, but his expression is one that old Santiago would have recognized. It's somewhere between calm and calculated, but I don't even care at this point.

"Why are you letting your girlfriend get followed around like that?" Carmen asks, bumping my side as she stands next to me and watches as Brooklynn continues walking, her entourage close behind.

"Why are you so concerned with my relationship?" I reply.

"Wow, I guess *that's* a touchy subject. Seriously, though, go shoo those guys away from her." Carmen says, sounding slightly annoyed. I'm not sure why she's this interested, but to be fair, less than a week ago, I was photographed by every news outlet, by her side on the red carpet, so me not being glued to her side might seem strange.

"It's not a touchy subject, it's just that we're..." I trail off for a moment as I try to find the right words for our current situation that still allude to the idea that we're together, but Carmen doesn't even let me think before she starts talking again.

"Santiago! If you're about to tell me that you broke up with her, I will be so done with you." She says more than a little bit threateningly, and her outburst catches me off guard.

"First, why are you assuming that *I* broke up with her? Second, we're not broken up." I retort quickly, not wanting Carmen to start spinning this false narrative.

"Well, to answer number one, you've always been the heartbreaker in your relationships, right? And second, if you're not broken up, why are you staring at her like she's carrying your heart in her hands?" Carmen replies just as quickly.

"What, so now that you're in a relationship, you're the relationship expert or something?" I ask, looking her up and down before doing the same to Alessandro. "Also, yes, maybe I have been the one who ends relationships in the past, but none of that has anything to do with Brooklynn. My relationship with her is nothing like anyone in the past." I defend, not liking how I'm quickly becoming the target of this situation.

"Oh, he's in *love*." Carmen giggles, leaning her head into Alessandro's chest, as though I'm not even here anymore.

"That's not-"

"Oh, he *definitely* is," Alessandro smirks, wrapping his arm around Carmen's shoulder, as he gives me a glance.

"Hey, let's not talk about my relationships right now. You're both about to be late for your classes." I huff, adjusting my school bag, flustered with this entire conversation.

"Ooh, now he's ending the entire conversation, too. He's *so* in love." Carmen giggles again, kissing Alessandro's hand before turning to her classroom, leaving Alessandro and I to walk to our class together. Great.

We start walking in the direction of our class, and while I'm not purposely ignoring him, I'm also not going to be starting a conversation with him right now.

"Hey, Santiago, can we talk later or something?" Alessandro says, just as we reach the large wooden door for our class. I don't turn to face him, as I'd like to leave this as casual as possible and not act like I'm still mildly frustrated with him and Carmen, but I nod my head.

"Yeah, but it will have to be quick, because I have stuff to do after school is out."

"That's fine, I-"

"Do you expect the rest of us to just wait for you while you talk?" Mrs. Hart asks, even though it's clearly not a question. She's tapping her shoe as she waits, and I glance at the clock above her head and see that we're almost five minutes late. Here at Blackstone, that's basically like saying you want to fail the class and never graduate.

"Of course not." Alessandro and I say at the same time, quickly entering and closing the door as we take our seats.

"Since everyone is finally here, let's begin." And with that, I remove any thoughts that might distract me from learning, but there's one that doesn't leave, no matter how hard I try.

Brooklynn.

"Hey, Santiago?" Alessandro's voice is behind me as I stride through the parking lot, and my agreement to talk to him resurfaces.

"Yes?"

"Sorry, I thought you forgot that we were going to talk for a moment." You would be right.

"Nope. What do you need?" My tone isn't rude, but I'm definitely not sugarcoating it, either.

"I just wanted to say that even though we haven't really talked, I'm sorry for not telling you that Carmen and I were dating. Regardless of what happened in the past—are we fully past that?—I should have said something instead of participating in deliberately hiding our relationship from you." Alessandro apologizes. His voice and words are genuinely sincere, and to be honest, I'm actually surprised.

"I accept your apology, but just so you know, it's really annoying to only find out that your little sister is dating your friend when they kiss right in front of you." Sucking in a deep breath, I continue. "I'm past it with you. At this point, I don't even care, because I was basically the whole problem." Alessandro's face looks like I've taken a thousand bricks off his shoulders.

"Really? I did play a part in-"

"What are you guys doing?" Carmen asks as she reaches our car. I turn, having forgotten that our driver has been waiting for me to get in the car.

"What does it look like? Talking." Although my words would usually sound harsh, Carmen can tell that I'm just messing with her, and she rolls her eyes and smiles before climbing in.

"Hey, no goodbye?" Alessandro teases, quickly stepping over to the open door and leaning his head in.

"Just because I forgave you doesn't mean that I want all of this public display of affection all in my face." I call out. Alessandro laughs as he walks past me, clapping my shoulder as he does so.

"That's funny, coming from someone who's in every news headline right now because of your public display of affection with your girlfriend." He yells back, already a few cars away.

"Ah, so you're keeping up with me that closely. I see how it is!" I yell back.

"I can't escape it if I tried! You're everywhere!" He shouts back. I don't even bother replying, since he's too far away now, but I do chuckle to myself as I climb into my seat. Alessandro is already acting like nothing happened, which, even just a month ago, would have really annoyed me, but now, I'm actually really glad.

"What's all of this about?" Carmen inquires, her curiosity obviously intrigued.

"What do you mean?"

"You know what I mean. That." She waves her hand at me, and then at the window of the car. "You and Alessandro are acting like best friends or something."

"Don't forget, he was my best friend before he was your boyfriend." I tease. All Carmen does is shake her head in disbelief, but she doesn't question me anymore.

CHAPTER 30

Brooklynn

As I'm leaving school, I spot Santiago and Alessandro talking near his car, and I almost do a double-take. Weren't they just on non-speaking terms? What's the switch about? I guess Carmen dating him has something to do with it, but Santiago used to act like he'd rather die than be friends with him again. He also used to act like he wasn't going to break my heart, but here we are.

"Brooklynn, Marie reached out to me about wanting to schedule a meeting with you sometime this week," Mom says as I walk through the living room after I get home. She's seated on one of the large sofas, a cup of tea in one hand, a book in the other. Everything about her radiates peace and love, and for a moment, I just want to swap lives with her and enjoy the perfect calmness that lives within her.

"Okay, I'll call her tomorrow and get something set up," I say, already dreading the meeting. Of course, I have nothing against Marie, but the meetings themselves always come with lots of decisions, talking, and overall stress. Yes, I know that all jobs have that, but that doesn't mean I have to like it.

"That sounds good, sweetie. Are you okay? You look a little bit tired." There's a hint of worry in her voice, but again, her softness doesn't allow it to dominate her tone.

"I'm just super tired, and after all of this new fame, I've been getting a lot of attention at school," I say this carefully, but she already knows what I mean.

"So there are boys who won't leave you alone?"

"Well...yes. There are some girls, but there are a lot of boys." I admit.

"I'll talk to your dad about it, because we've already been considering sending a bodyguard with you to school. He's been worried about this for a while now, and said that it was practically a matter of time until it was completely necessary." Mom explains.

"Okay. It's not a huge problem right now, but it's just draining."

"Yes, I do know. Why don't you take a nap, and then we can all discuss it at dinner later." Mom suggests, with a bright smile on her face.

"That sounds good, thanks."

"No problem. Make sure you're down here by seven. I told him seven-fifteen, but you never know." Mom says absently, taking a sip of her tea.

"Who are you talking about?" I question, thrown off guard by her comment.

"Santiago, of course. I invited him for dinner, that way your dad and I can get to know him outside of all of that

New York crazy." Mom replies, as though she hasn't just dropped a bombshell on me.

"You invited him to dinner?" I question, like asking again will change her answer.

"Yes, honey. I invited Santiago Alvarez to come eat dinner with us." Mom says slowly, like her speed is the problem. "Is there a problem with that?"

"No, not at all. I was just confused and didn't realize we were having company for dinner." I quickly reply, giving her a smile before leaving the room and heading up into my bedroom.

How in the world am I going to sit at the same table as him, when all in less than a week we've kissed, and then basically broken up. There's no guidebook on how to handle your fake relationship, which then turned into real feelings, that then turned into a breakup.

"Santiago, thank you so much for coming on such short notice." Mom calls out as one of the housekeepers opens the door and lets him in. I know that if I don't go and greet him that Mom will definitely be suspicious, so I follow close behind her. After she gives him a quick hug, I do the same, and that's where mistake number one for the night happens.

If it's even possible, Santiago must have done something to smell even better than he did the last time I was close to him. But even worse than that, Santiago looks completely comfortable, as though being this close to me doesn't have any effect on him. Fine then. Two can play at this game.

"Nice to see you, Brooklynn." Santiago says as we walk into the dining room, the sparkly chandelier casting small rays of light on his face. The shadows on his face are highlighted by them, and for a moment, all I want to do is stare at him and take in the beauty that he radiates.

Snap out of it, Brooklynn. He doesn't want you.

"Nice to see you, too," I say politely, taking my seat, which is unfortunately right across from him. Yay.

After the food has been brought out and everyone has their plates, while Dad says a prayer, I take Santiago's hand, trying to keep my thoughts far away from him.

"So, Santiago, how was celebrity life for you in New York?" Dad asks a few minutes later, practically oblivious to the tension between Santiago and me.

"It was interesting, that's for sure. I can say, for a fact, you're crazy for being in the acting business for so long." Santiago says jokingly, and Dad chuckles.

"To me, everything except for the acting is business. However, I love the acting so much that I'm willing to look past all of that extra stuff." Dad replies. "Although it is pretty nice to get my beautiful wife dressed up and show her off to the world." He says with a wide smile, resting his hand on her thigh.

"Oh, come on," Mom says with a laugh, but she's smiling ear to ear, and I know she doesn't actually mind it. Santiago watches emotionless for a second before plastering a bright smile on his face, as though he remembered it as a formality, not like he's genuinely amused by my dad's answer. That's weird.

"Brooklynn has been having trouble with the boys at school recently." Mom suddenly says, very pointedly looking at Santiago as she does so. If I could just evaporate, I would absolutely do so right now. The only thing that could keep me here would be watching Santiago's reaction, because he's even more uncomfortable than I am, and that just about makes this whole evening worth it. Almost.

"She has? Brooklynn, what's this about?" Dad asks, concern seeping into his voice.

"Well, a lot of boys have been bothering me and following me around," I say carefully, not fully sure why Mom decided to bring this up now. Santiago's hand clenches his fork so tightly that I almost wonder if he's going to break the gold cutlery. His knuckles are turning white from the pressure, and I'm sure he's just as uncomfortable as I am, hence his reaction.

"We're going to handle this, don't worry. I'm sure you've had more female attention since you were seen with Brooklynn, right, Santiago?" Mom asks, and for the first time ever, Santiago actually looks embarrassed. Maybe this dinner was a good idea.

"Well, yes, but I'm sure it's nothing like what Brooklynn has been going through. I'm too busy to notice them." He stammers out. Good. At least he's not paying them any attention. Not that I would have a problem if he were, but it's good that he's not.

The rest of the evening drags on with not much happening, the only mildly interesting thing being Santiago making eye contact with me at least seven different times, which, at this point—we've literally made out before—isn't much. After he's left and I'm in my room, I feel my frustration with him building up again, because, unfortunately, I definitely still like him. The only problem with that is that he obviously doesn't like me, and I'm not going to be doing anything about my feelings, since he just acted like nothing happened. I can't put myself out there if he doesn't want me.

CHAPTER 31
Santiago

I want her so much it hurts.

That's the only coherent thought I have on my drive home, and it echoes off the walls of my mind as the streetlights pass by at an exceedingly fast pace.

How is it even possible to want someone this much? I thought seeing her from afar at school was bad enough, but here I am, still in some sort of shock, after breathing in her scent and hearing her soft voice as she sat just mere feet from me.

I *need* her.

I'm not sure how it has taken me this long to realize that I need her, but it's been too long. Starting tonight, I'm going to do everything in my power to make her mine. For real this time. Nothing fake. Nothing out of ulterior motive. Nothing other than the fact that I need Brooklynn, and I've been so stupid in not realizing it sooner. How did I make out with her and act like I could move on from it, since I didn't know how she felt? How was I so close to her—both emotionally and physically—and still oblivious to the fact that *I. Need. Her.*

"Where have you been, and why do you look so rough?" Matteo asks as I walk down the hall, past his room, towards mine. Of course he's still awake to see the pure craziness that I'm feeling. "Santiago?" Well, there's no avoiding him now.

"Yes?" My voice is about as calm as I can make it in my current situation, but that's not nearly enough to throw Matteo off.

"Come in here for a minute, would you? I've been wanting to talk about something with you." Matteo says a moment later, as though he's been considering something. Curiosity gets the better of me, and I walk into his room, the door swinging slightly closed as I do so.

"What's going on?" I ask, sitting in the recliner near his desk, Matteo turning his chair to face me.

"Well, first, I think we need to address the obvious." He says point blank, staring me in the face.

"About?" I play stupid, but we both know exactly what he's talking about.

"Your little New York trip with Brooklynn Carmine," Matteo says, this time sounding less like an older brother and more like a friend. He's always been able to do this. He's always had the ability to go from being a person of authority to someone you can tell anything to.

"She asked me to start fake-dating her the day I met her, the last day of August, and then things kind of spiraled." I admit, not even trying to hide it from him. If there's only one person that I can't lie to, it's Matteo.

"And now?" He questions, knowing that there's obviously more to the story.

"Well things went well, and then most of September she was busy and we didn't see each other much, then in October we got really close, which then led to me going to the premiere for her movie, since her co-star was there and she was having a little bit of media trouble with him." The words are starting to tumble out of my mouth, and hearing myself talk about it all is almost therapeutic.

"After that?" Matteo is thoroughly invested and wants all of the details, which at this point, I don't mind talking about.

"Just so we're clear, I didn't have feelings for her even then. Well, that I was really aware of." I start, needing to get that out in the open before continuing. "Then on the last night we were there, I was feeling high on the whole trip. Something about being so close to her all week, being her comfort and strength, was intoxicating, and I wasn't thinking that night." Matteo's face pales as I speak, and I hurry to finish my story before he thinks the absolute worst of me. "So we got back to the hotel and ended up going to the rooftop hot tub, where we kissed."

"Oh." Is Matteo's response, since he was expecting much worse. "Just kissed?"

Does he want me to lay out every detail of the best make-out I've ever had? "We made out, if that's what you're asking. Nothing more than that, of course." He visibly releases a breath, and if the situation weren't about Brooklynn and me, this would seriously be comedic. "But then when we went to our rooms, she practically slammed the door in my face, and then we didn't talk for the next two days."

"You did *what?*" Matteo's voice is horrified, and I'm beginning to worry that he's getting the wrong idea of what happened.

"We didn't go in the same room or anything, it wasn't-"

"You didn't *talk* to her the next day? After you *made out* with her in a *hot tub.*" Something clicks, and it all falls into place. Even though I was sure she didn't like me after that, I still should have done something, regardless of my feelings at the time.

"Matteo, you're right. I let her just assume, and didn't say or do anything. How could I be so stupid?" Everything falls into place as her odd behavior those next few days flit through my mind. She wasn't angry at me. She was hurt.

"Of course I'm right. Although I wish I weren't. So, what happened to make you look like you did when you walked in here earlier?"

"I had dinner with her family." I say the words as calmly as possible, but when talking about the girl I completely messed everything up with, it's rather difficult to do that.

"And?"

"And she acted like I wasn't there, and only acknowledged me when I first got there, or when our eyes met. Matteo, I've been through some hard things, but I think this was the actual worst." I admit, disliking how weak I sound.

"So she still has feelings for you?" Matteo questions, although he says it more like a statement.

"I hope so."

"You need to do something, Santiago. If you really like her, then you need to fix this." His voice is both comforting and stern.

"That's why I looked so rough earlier. I made up my mind on the way home that I *will* make things right. I want Brooklynn *so* badly." My voice wavers ever so slightly, but I force strength back into it as I continue. "I have hope that she still likes me, but I'm going to do this right, and be her *real* boyfriend. No more made-up stories or fake dates. It will all be real now." Matteo smiles at this, and it's so unlike his usual one that it catches me off guard. "What?" I finally ask

"I'm just happy for you." He says simply.

"Happy that I'm in this position?" I half joke, still so confused.

"Happy that you've found someone who makes you feel this way. I know you love Carmen and me, but that's a different emotion. You've never felt like this for anyone else, and I'm happy that you're finally getting to experience this." Matteo explains, his eyes shifting for a moment.

"Thank you, but let's save the congratulations until after I have the girl of my dreams." I say with a smile, leaning my head back for a moment before remembering something. "Hey, what were you going to tell me? When I first came in here, you said you wanted to talk about something." Matteo's face shifts slightly, but he clears his throat.

"I wanted to talk to you about...*my* relationship." Matteo's relationship? "As you may or may not know, Daniela is back in town." Daniela Lozano. "And, given our history, it wasn't long before we got involved again."

Matteo's voice sounds strained, and I know how hard this is to talk about. Especially with me.

"That's good, right?" I ask. I'm not as good as Matteo at getting people to talk, but I want to be here for him. I need to be here for him after everything that I've put him through.

"Yes, of course it's good, but she just keeps telling me that it's casual, and we're good friends. She also has a different guy trying to win her over." He takes a deep breath. "Santiago, I've taken her out and made it painstakingly obvious that I'm still in love with her, but she's refusing to fully open up to me." *In love.* I don't think I've ever heard Matteo say those words before—probably because Daniela is the only girl he's ever dated—and it's almost strange.

"Well, that's...hard." My ability to hold an emotionally vulnerable conversation with anyone other than Brooklynn needs to be studied, because I just sound insensitive at this point. "What I mean is, maybe you need to outright tell her that you still love her?" I quickly amend. Even still, my words are more of a question, whereas Matteo was sure of his advice when he was listening to me.

"Do you actually think I should do that?" Matteo is genuinely interested in my opinion, and it feels like I'm about to start sweating at any given moment. Am I really qualified to give this kind of advice? I'm the reason they broke up in the first place.

"Matteo, I'm obviously not good at this stuff—look at the Brooklynn situation—but my honest advice is that she wouldn't be surprised to hear that you're still in love with her, and it's sounding like time is ticking. What's the worst that happens if she rejects you? You've already been through this once." Wow, that's the most solid piece of advice I've ever given.

"Santiago, you don't understand. I can't deal with it if she doesn't want me. If I tell her I love her and she doesn't say anything back to me..." He trails off like he'll be able to find the perfect analogy, but I know he won't. Matteo will never have an analogy to how he feels for Daniela. Matteo feels for Daniela like she's the only woman on earth, and he would live a thousand lives before looking away from her.

"I get it—kind of—but Matteo, this might be your last chance to have a relationship with her."

"I know, I know," Matteo says, raking his hands through his hair, leaning back in his chair like this is one of his business problems that he just needs to rest his eyes from. "Thank you, Santiago. It was good to get this all out there, and you know, talk about it with someone."

"Yeah," Is all I reply. Walking into my room and flopping into bed, I contemplate our conversation. It's been years since I've felt genuinely close to Matteo, and even just two months ago, I wouldn't have had this kind of conversation with him. What's changed?

Brooklynn.

I know for a fact that Brooklynn has something to do with it, because I found myself becoming more and more open with her, sharing things that even I didn't want to admit to myself.

Who would have thought that a girl from the other side of the country would have shifted my life this much? What if she hadn't boldly walked up to me that night at the party, asking about Alessandro? What if she ended up with him, instead of her with me, and Carmen and Alessandro? Well, she's not mine yet, but still. For a moment, a smile forms on my face as I picture Kai, almost thankful for him causing all of these problems, creating the need for her to have a fake relationship.

Fake relationship. She initiated our fake relationship, and now I'm going to initiate our real one. One where she'll never have to guess if I actually like her, or if any of it is real. Every second of it will be real, even if that slightly scares me. I can't get this wrong, and the only way to do that is to be open and honest about my feelings and to answer everything she asks with the truth. While I never lied to Brooklynn about anything, I would intentionally dodge her questions when things got uncomfortable, and maybe that's one of the things that convinced Brooklynn I didn't like her.

My last coherent thoughts before I fall asleep are that no matter what, even if Brooklynn rejects me, she will know how I feel.

"Hey, come on, we've barely seen you this month," Lyle calls out as I turn my back to him and the rest of the group. His words cause anger to shoot through my veins, and I turn to face him. I don't know why agreeing to see them before the party at The Enchanted Ivy sounded like a smart idea, but something takes over me, and I decide that I'm done with this.

"Yeah, you're right about that." I take a step closer, feeling the heat seep through my body. "And do you know why?" The golf course lights illuminate the rest of our group around us, but I single Lyle out as I speak.

"Why?" Lyle challenges back, taking a step closer to me. My eyebrows flick at his sudden boldness, but I don't hesitate.

"Because most of you, especially you, are so childish, and cause more problems than anything else in my life." I hiss, finally being honest with both him and myself. I'm not sure why it's taken me this long to realize it, but being around my group of friends leaves me in a worse mood than I began in, and they're always up to trouble.

That's not to say that I've never been the cause of trouble, but I can pretty confidently say that I haven't been the instigator for a long time. A *very* long time.

"How dare you-"

"How dare I admit that you're one of the most insufferable people in the entire world? How dare I admit that all of the things you find fun and exciting are *stupid*? How dare I admit that you act like such a leader, but if in the lurch, you'll leave all of your 'friends' in an instant?" I shoot back, the words tumbling from my mouth as I let out the words that have sat near the back of my mind for months.

"If you're just intimidated by me, say it, Santiago. We all know that when it comes down to it, *you're* the one who would leave your friends. Just like how as soon as you met that girl, you decided you were done with us."

"Maybe that's because she showed me that I can have fun without being stupid."

"Maybe it's because you're so obsessed with her and she has *other* ideas of fun."

"Don't. You. Dare." I snarl, hating how Lyle didn't just

bring Brooklynn into this, but now he's insulting her, too. "I'm leaving. Once and for all. I want nothing to do with you, and I want you to stay away from Brooklynn."

"Or what?" Lyle taunts, my anger a game to him, now.

"You don't want to know." I say through a clenched jaw, the words sounding deep and threatening.

"So not only are you insulting me, you're also going to threaten me as well?" Lyle demands, but some of the fire has left his eyes as he realizes that I'm not even slightly joking.

"Yes, I am. And that goes for all of you. No one is to harass Brooklynn, and you better pass that message along at school, as well." I say sharply, my eyes meeting each and every set of eyes around us, landing on Lyle as I finish.

"Well, it appears that Santiago is too good for us now. Let's go, guys." Lyle says, weakly trying to sound in control as he storms off the course, all but one of our 'friends' following him. Damon.

"Santiago, for the record, I agree with you. Thank you for finally putting Lyle in his place." Damon says, falling into step with me as we walk to the parking area. He won't be attending tonight's party, but our cars are parked near each other.

"You don't need to thank me. I need to get on with my life and grow, and running around with this group isn't the way to do it. Lyle just pushed me over the edge when he wouldn't stop. I never planned on everything going down like that." I admit, clapping Damon's shoulder as we reach the spot where we'll go our separate ways.

"I'm glad you did it for you. I guess I'll see you around sometime." Damon says with a nod. "Have fun, Santiago." And with that, he's driving out of the parking lot.

I know that he's probably not going to stop joining in on all of Lyle's crazy ideas, but out of everyone, he's the most likely to grow a backbone and leave Lyle's idiocy. I'm just glad I finally did.

My steps are lighter as I enter the main doors, like the invisible checklist only has one more thing to do. Alessandro and I are friends again, Matteo and I are acting like brothers, and I've rid myself of the last people who will be attaching me to the lifestyle I've been leaving behind. The only thing left to do is apologize to Brooklynn and hope that she gives me a second chance.

CHAPTER 32

Brooklynn

Walking into The Enchanted Ivy feels like walking into a ballroom from a hundred years ago. The autumn decorations fill the room, and everything from the curtains to the lights has been changed to fit the autumn theme. Tonight is more of a ball than a party, and all of the women are dressed in long, flowing dresses, with the men in their tuxedos. Glancing down at my dress for the second time tonight, I check it over as if it has suddenly changed shape and doesn't fit the dress code anymore. Nope. It's still the same long, red dress with endless ruffles and intricate stitching.

"Brooklynn, right?" A male voice asks near my ear, causing me to startle as I look up. The boy talking to me looks about a year or so older than me, with dirty blond hair and a sharp jawline.

"Hello," I say, taking his extended hand and shaking it. "Yes, I'm Brooklynn." My confusion must be obvious as I glance over his face for anything recognizable, but I'm pretty sure I've never seen this man before.

"Oh, sorry, how rude of me. My name is Marcus." He—Marcus—says, his icy blue eyes gazing into mine as he speaks. There's something both comforting and chilling about them, as though they balance each other out perfectly.

"It's lovely to meet you, Marcus. Is there something I can help you with?" I ask with a smile, curious as to why he came over to me in the first place. Marcus smiles and looks down before meeting my eyes again, as though he's not quite sure what to say.

"Oh, about that. I just had to come over and meet you after seeing you. When you came in earlier, you immediately intrigued me." Marcus admits, small dimples forming on his cheeks as he smiles. I blush at his words; something about Marcus' straightforwardness is attractive. Maybe not attractive in the sense that I like him, but it's definitely something I admire.

"Thank you. I guess I didn't see you earlier." I reply, slightly flustered, but more unsure of what to do. Marcus *is* trying to flirt with me, right?

"Don't flatter me. Even if you had seen me, you wouldn't have been as intrigued as I was when I saw you." Marcus says, and for a moment, I just stare into his blue eyes as I scramble for something to say.

"Do you come here often?" Is the first thing that comes to mind, and it seems like a safe topic in this conversation.

"No, actually. This is my first time here. My brother and I attend university near here, and our parents—they live in New York—insisted on finding us someplace to enjoy noncurricular activities." I blink at his answer, not because it's an odd reason, but because it was so straight and to the point that it sounded strange.

"Oh really? So, do you play golf or tennis?" I search my brain for a list of the many activities The Enchanted Ivy offers, and those are the only two that come to mind. I know there are plenty of other ones, but none are coming to mind.

"Both, actually. What about you?" Marcus responds easily, gazing intently into my eyes as he waits for a response.

"Well, I've played both quite a few times, but I wouldn't say that they're something I actually do on a somewhat regular basis," I answer truthfully. The lights dim just a little, and we both turn to see each other more clearly, but something catches my eye. Or, *someone.*

Santiago is standing at the top of the indoor balcony, staring directly at me, as though there isn't a crowd of people in the room. Like I'm the only person in the world. I meet his gaze, his face expressionless as he watches me. If this were anyone else, I would be completely creeped out by the thought of someone watching me, but with Santiago, I'm merely curious. Why is his attention fixed on me?

"Brooklynn?" Marcus' voice interrupts my thoughts, and I immediately feel stupid, because it's obvious he's been talking.

"I'm so sorry, I just got a little bit distracted. What did you say?" I say sheepishly. Marcus smiles at this, and I'm grateful he isn't offended by my rudeness.

"I said that maybe you would like to come with me sometime to go golfing, since you haven't been in a while." I smile, even though inwardly, I'm not too sure about this idea.

"That sounds fun. Maybe sometime our schedules will align." I say vaguely, not wanting to just say no—there's not really any way to do that—but also not wanting to say yes.

"You're an actress, right?" Marcus asks, his eyes fixed on mine as he speaks.

"I am. Who told you?" I reply with a laugh, unsure of who told him my name and what I do.

"There was another woman here, Daniela, I think, who told me I should talk to you." I raise my eyebrows at this because why would she just tell him to talk to me?

"Really?" I ask, somewhat skeptically, my voice still teasing.

"Well," Marcus says sheepishly, I asked her who you were and what your name was when I first saw you, because she was near me, and I figured she knew you." He rubs the back of his neck and grins, the combination of actions actually pretty cute.

"Ah, I see. What else did she say about me?" I tease.

"Well, she did say that you're really nice, and I shouldn't be worried about approaching you," Marcus admits.

"Am I?" I ask with a smile.

"Are you what?" Marcus questions, sounding slightly flustered.

"Am I nice and approachable?"

"Oh, well, of course." Marcus stammers, his smile and dimples returning. "Why?"

"Just wondering if I'm living up to your expectations." I tease, brushing a few curls off my shoulder and looking back up at him. While I consider Santiago tall, Marcus is *tall*. He's probably at least four or five inches taller than Santiago, which is over a foot taller than me.

"You, um, definitely live up to the expectations. More, even." Marcus quickly adds on.

"I'm teasing you, don't worry. I need to make sure the Brooklynn charm still works." I joke with a wink. Marcus' face flushes, and I immediately wish I hadn't done that. He's not Santiago. I can't just tease him like this and expect him to understand me. "So, are you here with anyone other than your brother?" I ask, quickly changing the topic.

"No, actually. I just started college this semester, and so far we've been so busy with studies." Marcus answers a little bit too eagerly.

"I'm in school here at Blackstone, so I understand being busy with studies. What's your brother's name? I don't think I've seen him." I reply.

"Well, you didn't notice me, so you probably wouldn't have noticed Rhys." Marcus teases, leaning slightly against the wall, as though he knows something I don't.

"Hey, just because I didn't notice you doesn't mean I wouldn't have eventually. But why wouldn't I have noticed him?"

"Fair enough, fair enough," Marcus concludes, crossing his arms. "You wouldn't have noticed him because we're identical twins."

"Really? That's pretty cool." I say, genuinely meaning it. "Wait, what if you're Rhys, and Marcus is somewhere else here?" I joke, raising my eyebrows in challenge.

"Wow, you're already accusing me of switching, when most people don't think of asking that until knowing us for a little bit longer," Marcus says with a laugh, clearly amused by how quickly I thought to ask that. "But rest assured that you're talking to Marcus, not Rhys." He amends. We talk for a few more minutes, but my eyes are wandering from him as I glance around the room for the tenth time. It's not that I'm not enjoying Marcus' company, but it's becoming increasingly obvious that he is trying to flirt, and I'm really not interested in him.

"Brooklynn, would you like to dance?" A voice I'd recognize anywhere asks from behind me. Santiago's cool, deep tone is both comforting and surprising. I turn to face him, my breath catching as my eyes move over his face. Something about Santiago always leaves me speechless, and I don't think anything will ever change that.

"Yes." The traitorous words slip from my lips before I can say no, and I immediately want to smack my hand over my mouth. Why did I just say yes? Santiago smiles, and it's a genuine smile. Not the perfectly poised one he gives to most people, but the real one that I usually only see when we're alone. He extends his hand out to mine, and I place mine in his. For a moment, I'm in a daze. That is, until a voice clears his throat behind me, and I remember that Marcus is still standing there. Oops.

"Your dress is beautiful." Santiago says as we step to the middle of the floor, other couples around us dancing. "*You're* beautiful." He amends, gazing directly into my eyes as he speaks. Something about his eyes draws me in, and no matter how hard I try, they keep my attention.

"T-thank you. You're rather handsome, yourself." I admit, not having the heart to deny it. How am I so easily slipping back to being enraptured with Santiago?

"Thank you, Brooklynn." He says, spinning me, then wrapping his arm securely around my waist. Something about his touch, even if there are layers of dress between us, sends goosebumps up my back and shoulders. Closing my eyes for a brief moment, I remind myself that we're just dancing, and there's no reason to be acting this way.

"Why did you ask me to dance?" I find myself asking, the curiosity in me unable to contain itself. Santiago presses his lips together as if he's considering something, but he blinks and starts speaking.

"I was jealous." He admits, not even sounding slightly embarrassed.

"Jealous? Of what?" I question.

"Of whoever you were talking to over there. He looked like he was about to ask you to dance, and I knew that I wanted to dance with you." Santiago says this like it's a completely normal thing to say, and I raise my eyebrows at him.

"You thought Marcus was going to ask me to dance, and you had to do it first?"

"When you say it like that, it sounds strange, but yes. I've been wanting to ask you for the past half-hour, and what better time than now?" Santiago replies. What's with this new, open and honest Santiago?

"Why?" Is all I ask, blinking slowly as I watch him. Something is different about him today. He seems...free? I'm not sure if that's the right word, but he seems less uptight than he usually is.

"Because I regret it, and I'm sorry." Santiago replies, as though that's a complete answer.

"Because you regret what?"

"I regret being a jerk, and I regret wasting all of my time with you."

"You regret spending time with me?" I ask, reeling from his words, which he said completely casually.

"No, no. I meant I regret spending so much time with you, but never trying to be something more than just your fake boyfriend. I did all you asked of me, but nothing more, and I regret spending all of that time not doing more for you." Where is this even coming from?

"That's..." I trail off, unsure of what to even say. "You were everything I asked for, Santiago. You didn't have to do anything else."

"But I *wanted* to do more. I wanted you to be more." Santiago says quietly, meeting my eyes as he speaks. "I regret acting like the only reason I was there was because you wanted me."

"What do you mean?" I whisper.

"I mean that I wanted you, too." Santiago says clearly, his voice smooth and calm as he speaks. It doesn't even sound right in my head, because even though I only wanted him in a fake way then, I still wanted him so much more than I'll ever admit.

"Why are you telling me all of this now?" I finally ask. Just as I'm deciding to move past the hurt I feel from him ignoring me after the best kiss I've ever had, he's now deciding to say this.

"Because I have regrets, and I can't go any longer without telling you that."

"Santiago, it's only been a few days since we agreed to part ways." I'm not sure why I'm saying this, because it's not like there's a number of days that are supposed to pass before you work through your feelings, but I'm not sure what else to say. What do I want him to say?

"And those few days were too many. Can we…" He trails off like he doesn't know how to finish his sentence, his gaze sweeping the room before returning to mine. "Can we start again? From the very beginning? I know that's a lot to ask, but I want to try again."

"Try what again?" Even though I know what he's saying, I want to know what his version of starting from the beginning means.

"I want to date you for real, but I want to start from the beginning and do it the right way, with me initiating our dates, and with me being the one to work so hard at our relationship. You carried the burden of our fake relationship, and that wasn't fair." Santiago answers, sounding sure of himself. More sure than I've ever heard him.

"I…" Trailing off, I try to find the right words. "I would like that. But for the record, I was the one with the insane fake dating idea, and there was no benefit to you, so while I carried the *burden,* it was fully mine to carry. Don't blame yourself for that."

Santiago smiles, and it brings one of my own to my lips. The song ends before we can speak anymore, but right after we're off to the side of the people dancing to the next song, Carmen asks Santiago to dance with her, and I shoo him off, because I know their relationship might be slightly strained right now, with the Alessandro situation.

"So I take it you know that guy?" Marcus asks as I watch Santiago dance with Carmen. His voice slightly startles me, but I turn to face him with a smile.

"I do. I'm guessing you don't keep up with much celebrity gossip, then?" Marcus' face is confused, and I can almost hear the gears turning in his head.

"Not really, no. Why would you say that?"

"Santiago was with me on the red carpet of my movie premiere last week," I say, not sure how else to word it. I could say that he's my boyfriend, but that's not exactly true. I could say that he went as my friend, but that's also not true.

"Oh, that's nice. So you definitely know him." Marcus jokes, a knowing expression on his face.

"Yeah, I do. He was the first person I started hanging out with when I moved here a few months ago." The words bring a smile to my face as I remember all of the little adventures Santiago and I would go on together.

"If you don't mind me asking, are you two...dating?" Marcus approaches the question with caution, but I don't blame him for being curious.

"Kind of. We're still figuring it out." I answer honestly, meeting his eyes as I say this. This is as much truth as he's getting from me, and there's an understanding look in Marcus' eyes.

"I get it, Brooklynn." He says knowingly, smiling after he's finished speaking. We talk for a few more minutes before Marcus excuses himself, saying that he needs to find his brother and be on his way, since he has classes in the morning. I do too, of course, but I'm sure his college is farther away than my house.

"So, how serious are you and my brother?" Carmen asks, approaching me after their dance is over, Santiago across the room with Matteo, engaged in what seems to be a very serious conversation.

"Hello to you, too." I tease. "You steal my date, then ask questions about our relationship, all without even greeting me first," I say, wrapping my arms behind her shoulders, pulling Carmen into a hug.

"You two are good for each other, because that is totally something Santiago would have just said to me," Carmen says with a laugh.

"A match made in heaven," I reply with a smile. "And as for if we're serious, I don't know."

"I think there's more to your relationship than what you two are letting on, but to be fair, we had our own secrets when Alessandro and I started dating, so I don't blame you," Carmen says with a smile. "When everything is settled, I do want to know how you got my brother to walk a red carpet in New York with you, though."

"Oh, that was easy. Santiago is pretty easy to convince." I say, giggling as I remember when I first approached him with the whole fake boyfriend thing, and how everything continued spiraling after that. Carmen just watches me with a smile.

"See, that's why you're good for each other. Santiago has never been easy to convince of anything, and for you, he just smiles and follows along. I've seen *all* of the clips of you two together, and the way he does anything and everything for you as soon as he sees you need something is really sweet. That one video where he takes off his jacket so you can walk up the stairs has gone viral on social media, and I think you two might have your own fandom or something." Carmen says with a laugh.

"Wait, really? I've turned all of my social media off since the premiere." I admit, fighting the urge to open my phone and search the internet for the video.

"Really. I think every news article has written about it,

too. You two are a big deal." As Carmen speaks, I chew on my bottom lip, considering her words. Are people really that in love with Santiago and I? Was it a mistake to take him? I don't particularly like the idea of millions of other women swooning over Santiago, but at the time, it was the best idea to keep my reputation intact.

"That's...crazy." I finally say, truly meaning it.

"Hey, I need to get going. Matteo is driving me home—our parents always drive alone—and he told me that we needed to leave by midnight." Carmen abruptly says, her eyes focusing on the large grandfather clock across the room.

"No problem. Maybe we can get together soon and spend more time together?" I ask, Carmen pulling me into a quick hug as I speak.

"Yes, we definitely need to. I'm super busy with modeling for Daniela, and I'm sure you have a lot of acting stuff, but we can work something out." Carmen replies, nodding as she speaks. "Okay, I really have to go. Matteo is going to leave me to drive with that madman of a boyfriend you have." She says with a giggle before turning and walking to the exit of the room. Does she really think Santiago is a bad driver? Surely not, because from my experience, he's been nothing but careful.

"I see my sister left you all alone. I guess I need to fix that." Santiago says as he approaches me, tentatively wrapping his fingers around mine. I smile and wrap mine around his, stepping closer, our arms now touching.

"You could definitely do something about that. Do you want to drive me home? My parents won't be leaving for another few hours, and I'm pretty tired." I'm sure he'll be leaving soon, so I don't expect this to be a problem for Santiago.

"Yes. I was actually thinking about getting home, anyway, so this is perfect. Do you need to let your parents know?" Santiago replies, squeezing my hand lightly as he waits for my response.

"I'll let them know that I'm leaving, but I'm sure they'll be fine."

A few minutes later, Santiago is opening the passenger door of his car for me. While I know that it hasn't actually been that long since the last time we went on a drive together, this feels strangely nostalgic. Something about us being alone in the dark, with the night lights passing by, is comforting.

"Brooklynn?" Santiago's voice breaks the comfortable silence, and for a moment, I wonder if I imagined him speaking, since he only said my name.

"Yes?" I answer curiously.

"Thank you for giving me another chance. I'm sorry for not realizing that you were right there in front of me the whole time, and that I wasn't actively pursuing you. When you said we were over, it was like something in me shifted, because you weren't mine—fake or not—anymore, and there was nothing in the moment I could do that would change that." I'm not sure where this is all coming from, but it brings a small smile to my face as Santiago opens up about all of this, completely unprompted.

"I don't think I should be saying 'you're welcome' even though you said thank you, but I don't really know what else to say, besides the fact that I'm glad you really like me back. For a while, I was completely convinced you didn't like me, because you just kissed me, then never brought it up." The words come tumbling out of my mouth, and as I realize how harsh this sounds, Santiago's wince is enough to let me know that the words are cutting a little bit deep. "Sorry, that was-"

"No, you're right for feeling that way, because kissing you like that was so stupid, especially on the night of your movie premiere and everything. I don't regret kissing you, but the timing was completely off. I was so worried when you left that you didn't like me, and then I just ignored you." Santiago says immediately, as though he's been thinking about this for a while. Instead of saying anything, I reach over and take his hand, running my thumb along the back of his hand. "I want to do things the right way with you, Brooklynn." Although I hear the sincerity in his voice, there's a small part of me that's worried he's being rash. While I don't think he'd be telling me this if he didn't believe it himself, who's to say this isn't a moment of jealousy caused by seeing me with someone else?

Soon enough, we're at my house, and Santiago is opening my door for me at the gates. Since my parents didn't call ahead and tell security that I'd be arriving in a different vehicle, they're not allowed to let Santiago past. However, I can tell that they recognize him from our little escapades in the night, and him being over here for dinner the other night.

"Good night, Brooklynn." Santiago says as he helps me out of the car. Our eyes meet, and time stills for just a moment as I imagine we're just as we used to be. Without the uncertainty that we're in now. I take a step closer to Santiago, our toes nearly touching now, and gently but surely, I wrap my arms around him, bringing us into a hug.

Santiago is stiff for the slightest moment, but he quickly wraps his arms around me, resting his chin on the top of my head. His smell is something I didn't realize I've been missing until right now, and breathing in Santiago's scent propels me back to that night when he kissed me.

"Good night, Santiago. Thank you for bringing me home." I whisper into his chest, pressing my cheek against his heart. His body warmth is extremely nice in the cold night air, and it's almost as though the temperature isn't as low as it is. All I feel is his heat. Santiago's pulse quickens, and I smile against his tuxedo at the feeling of his heart beating faster. Santiago tightens his arms around me, and I know that he won't be the first one to pull away. Resting in his embrace for a moment longer, I step back. "Drive safely, okay?"

Santiago's face is soft, and it's an expression that I only see when it's just the two of us. For a moment, he doesn't respond, and he continues gazing into my eyes. "I will. Sleep well." He finally says, waiting for me to walk inside the gates and onto the lit pathway to the house before he gets in his car.

Once I'm inside my bedroom, I find myself slipping to the floor, resting against the door as the events of this evening play in my mind. Wrapping my arms around my knees and allowing my head to drop to them, the feeling of Santiago's arms around me still lingers, and I can almost imagine that he's right here with me. His scent, warmth, and feeling, all consuming me.

CHAPTER 33

Santiago

My body is on fire as I sit in my car, hoping to regain some sort of control over myself before I start driving. I had no idea that Brooklynn possessed this much control over me, but here I am, completely a wreck after she hugged me and pressed her head into my chest like we've done that a million times. Like I didn't stop breathing, in hopes of her leaving her head there for just a moment longer.

"So, am I allowed to ask about your relationship?" Alessandro asks as he strides next to me on our last class of the day. I glance over at his curious expression, and a small smile forms on my face. How did we go years without talking? Of course, nobody can replace my actual brother, but there was a moment in time, I was closer to Alessandro than I was to Matteo, and I can easily see how that happened. We get along so well, and we get each other in a way that's similar to the relationship I have with Matteo. I swallow, remembering all of the unanswered messages and calls on my phone from Lyle and the rest of my 'friends,' and it's obvious to me which of my friendships I'm favoring more.

"I guess. What do you want to know?" This is our longest walk in school, since we have to get from the very front of the school to the very back, which is easily almost a mile apart, due to the various hallways, so I actually don't mind passing the time with conversation.

"Well, I'm actually kind of curious about how Brooklynn and you became a thing. She must have met you right after she got here, right?" A laugh escapes me, and Alessandro's confused expression adds to the humor.

"Yeah, she did. Don't let this get to your head or anything, and definitely don't get any ideas, but the night we met, she came up to me, asking about you." Alessandro's eyebrows shoot up, completely unbelieving of my story.

"What are you talking about? Why was she asking about me?" Alessandro asks, his voice clearly confused, but also interested in the story. I end up laying everything out for him—besides the part where we kissed—and by the end of it, Alessandro can't even contain his laughter. "And here I was thinking the story behind how Carmen and I started dating was interesting. Which, if I'm remembering correctly, I met her the day after you met Brooklynn, if you're curious."

"Yeah, you could say that it hasn't been exactly the fairytale that we spun." I say, hoisting my backpack higher on my shoulder. "I guess it was a good thing for both of us that I still didn't like you back then. Imagine you with Brooklynn. Actually, don't imagine that." Alessandro just laughs.

"Yeah, I don't want to. I'm really happy with Carmen. It's like there's a different side to me that I didn't even know I had until I met her. Does that sound weird?" Alessandro confesses, sounding like he hasn't admitted this before. The strange thing is that I *do* know what he's talking about.

"I do. It might have sounded weird to me a few months ago, but I really do get it." I contemplate making Alessandro uncomfortable for a moment, and the opportunity is too good to pass up. "Although it is weird to hear you say that about my little sister." Alessandro's neck immediately flushes, and I can't hold in my laughter. "I think the best part about you dating Carmen is that one day you'll actually be my brother." I take a pause, and Alessandro looks relieved at the direction of the conversation. Too bad for him, because I'm not done yet. "And the fact that I'll be able to make you uncomfortable and tease you whenever I feel like it." The flush comes right back, but Alessandro is smiling now.

"I'm glad you have amusement for the rest of your life, then. We wouldn't want you to be running low on things that you find humorous, now would we?" Alessandro jokes back, elbowing me as we enter our classroom. "But for Carmen, I guess I'll put up with you." Of course, Alessandro had to get the last poke in, now that we can't talk. I smile, though, glad for our friendship.

Once class is over, I begin my search for Brooklynn. This morning, I saw her chatting with Carmen as they entered their classrooms, and other than arriving at school, we have just about no class periods that overlap.

"They're leaving room one hundred and three," Alessandro says, falling into step beside me as we exit our class.

"What?"

"Carmen and Brooklynn are leaving room one hundred and three. That's their last class of the day." He repeats. Of course, he knows Brooklynn's schedule, since it lines up with Carmen's. For a moment, I'm jealous of his knowledge, but I remind myself that he's been with Carmen for a few months now, and this was one of the few places that they were able to see each other at.

"So let's meet them. Are you doing anything else today?" I ask, bodies brushing by us as we walk in the direction of the girls' classroom.

"Yeah, we're going to get ice cream, and then something for Carmen," Alessandro responds easily.

"You're taking her shopping?" The thought of Alessandro taking Carmen shopping is slightly amusing because I know firsthand how pricy she can get. Alessandro smiles, as if reading my thoughts.

"Yep. Last time it was a bag, before that it was dresses, shoes, and the list goes on. But I don't spend much money by myself, so it's good that it's going to be used." Going to use. Alessandro justifying spending the money is even more funny. He is *really* wrapped around Carmen's finger, and he doesn't mind one single bit. Do I feel the same way about Brooklynn? Does she feel the same way about me? Do I know what I'm going to say when I see her in a few moments? Alessandro seems to already have his afternoon planned out, but I don't. Thinking quickly, I come up with a date idea for later, and as we near their hallway, I spot Brooklynn.

Her curls are pulled into a ponytail with a few strands out near her face, and her head is nodding vigorously as Carmen hangs on her arm, speaking rapidly about something Brooklynn obviously agrees on. From the way her hair bounces with each movement, to her beautiful eyes as she looks at Carmen, everything about her sends my heart beating erratically. They both notice us at the same time, with Carmen's eyes pure excitement as they land on Alessandro, and Brooklyn's curious as she meets my gaze. Her long eyelashes flutter as I approach her, as though she's curious, but not exactly sure what's happening.

"Hey, Santiago," Brooklynn says, smiling as I stop in front of her. "What's up?"

"Hey," I reply, suddenly unsure of myself as my mind becomes jumbled. Her eyes focusing on me as she peers through her eyelashes, her soft voice, and her smile, are causing some sort of malfunction in my brain, and anything cool that I planned to say seems to have evaporated.

"Did you have something you wanted to say?" She says, giving me an opening. It's now or never, I guess.

"Do you want to go out with me later today? On a date?" My last words sound like a question, and I force myself to get a grip. "I'd like to take you out on a date later, if you're available."

CHAPTER 34

Brooklynn

I blink twice, his upfront asking for a date is a surprise, since he never did this before. My immediate reaction is to say yes, but I remind myself to rein in my excitement. I can't get this excited when only last night did Santiago tell me that he wants me back. For all I know, this will last a week, with him deciding that fake dating me was the only fun part of our relationship, and actually dating me isn't interesting.

Saying yes is the reasonable thing to do, but I give him a moment before responding, just so he knows—or thinks—that I'm not desperate for his attention again. Santiago is slightly uncontrolled, as Daniela told me when she first spoke of him. While I don't think of that as a bad trait of his, I still have to remember how easily he jumped into the whole fake-dating thing, and how quickly he lost confidence in our relationship. The worst thing would be me getting my hopes up, and him not being ready to commit to a relationship.

"That sounds fun. What do you have planned?" I finally reply, not saying yes, but not saying no.

"Well, I was thinking we could go for a walk at The Enchanted Ivy, and maybe hang out around the pond at the golf course. Just something less stressful and with fewer—or no—people, since these last few weeks we haven't been able to just be around each other." Santiago explains, like he's planned it all out. It *does* sound fun.

"That actually sounds pretty nice. What time are you thinking?" Santiago beams.

"Seven-fifteen? We can go earlier if you'd like to get dinner, of course, but I didn't know if you had dinner plans." Santiago answers, as though he's regretting not asking me to dinner as well. I'm glad he didn't, because I don't think I'm ready just yet for that many hours alone with Santiago. That much time with just us will make me forget about needing to keep a safe amount of distance between us. It's not that I *don't* want Santiago, but more than I want him, I don't want to feel that rejected like I did when he kissed me, and the next day he didn't do anything. Even though it was a big misunderstanding between us, it still hurt.

"No, seven-fifteen is good. I have dinner with my parents, so don't worry about that." I respond, smiling as I imagine spending the evening with Santiago.

"So it's a date. I'll be at your house at seven-fifteen, then."

"I'm going to be leaving at seven to go out with Santiago." The statement pops out of my mouth as Mom and Dad sit down on the couch with me, since we just finished dinner a few minutes ago.

"Oh? That sounds fun." Mom says, flicking her eyebrows slightly, but no real signs of surprise on her face.

"Yeah, I think it will be," I reply, finishing a problem in my homework. Mom and Dad don't really care about my comings and goings, but I've made it a habit to usually let them know when I'm leaving. It's kind of our unspoken understanding that as long as I try to mention it, they don't mind.

"He's going to pick you up, right?" Dad asks, picking his head up from the screenplay he's reading. Dad doesn't act a lot anymore, but he still gets sent screenplays from his director friends, since they like hearing his opinion on them. I'm pretty sure it's also an indirect way of offering him a role, if he finds a character or story that he's particularly fond of.

"Yes, he'll be here at seven-fifteen." I hum, adding the last numbers to the answer I'm writing out.

"Sounds good. You might want to get ready, though. He'll be here in forty-five minutes." Dad says after checking his watch.

"I'm about to, I just need to finish this last page, then I'm done with homework."

Exactly forty-five minutes later, there's a knock on the door, and Dad glances over at me, as if to ask if he wants to know if I want him to get the door. I give him a nod, since this is technically a date.

"Hey, Santiago. How are you doing?" Dad asks, welcoming Santiago into the entryway.

"I'm doing well, how about you?" Santiago replies, shaking Dad's hand before turning to me. It's almost as though his eyes were in constant movement until they stopped on me, and now they're unmoving, taking in every inch of me with careful and concise precision. "You're beautiful, Brooklynn." Santiago says as I walk towards him. Something about how he says I'm beautiful, instead of saying I look beautiful, catches my attention, but I can't place my finger on exactly why.

"Thank you. You didn't dress too terribly, yourself." I say with a small laugh, and Santiago's smile stretches across his face.

"I'll take what I can get." Is all he says, glancing at Dad, as though he's getting his final permission before taking me out. Dad just nods, and a moment later, we're walking down the flowered and lit path to the driveway. "Your dress is really nice." Santiago says as we reach his car, and he reaches around me, opening the door.

"Thank you, I really like it, too," I reply, sliding into the seat, as Santiago softly and securely closes the door. I've been saving this dark blue midi dress for just the right occasion, and tonight feels like the right time.

"How was your evening?" Santiago asks once we're on the road, and it's my first time noticing that he might be nervous. Smiling to myself and turning to him, I take in his features before answering.

"It was fun. My parents and I had dinner, then I did some homework, and now..." I trail off, looking Santiago up and down. "Now I'm with you. That's usually pretty fun." I'm not exactly sure why I'm flirting with him like this, since I've never really done that with him before, but something within me can't help it.

"Those things sound interesting, but the last thing

sounded the most fun. In my personal opinion, of course." Santiago says, easily driving through the evening traffic, and within a few minutes, we're at The Enchanted Ivy. Surprisingly, there's not a single other car here, and I feel my eyebrows furrow in confusion.

"Shouldn't there be at least a few people here?" I ask, and Santiago shuts off the car, quickly coming around to my side, opening the door before responding.

"Usually, yes. But tonight, I called and asked that the staff close early, so it's just us, and whatever staff is still here." Santiago says proudly, offering his arm as I step out. My jaw drops.

"You rented out the whole club for us?" I gasp, completely taken by surprise.

"For *you*." Santiago corrects, closing the door behind me.

"You didn't need to do something this elaborate, you know? This is only our first date, and I don't know how you're going to be able to top this for our next one." I say, feeling like this is both too much, but also extremely enjoyable.

"Don't worry about how I'm going to do better, just have an amazing time, and that's all that matters." Santiago assures me, glancing down at my hand before gently wrapping his around mine. My skin prickles as he does this, and goosebumps race their way up my arm, reaching my neck and shoulders.

"We're going to have an amazing evening, Santiago," I say, squeezing his hand lightly as we begin walking one of the many paved paths that snake through the golf course.

"How have you been now that the movie stuff is behind

you?" Santiago asks a few minutes later, the only sounds other than him are coming from our footsteps, and the occasional bird call in the trees.

"Pretty good, actually. I love the whole process, and the premiere was fun, but I am glad that it's all behind me for now." I respond truthfully, thinking about how next month —if all goes to plan—I'll be in Europe for the start of filming for the travel romance Marie and I talked about. We agreed upon it the other day, and now all we need is the final word from the casting directors, and I'll be officially signed for the role.

"For now?" Santiago asks, sounding confused. I never did tell him about that, and my cheeks flush slightly.

"Well, next month, I should be flying to Europe for a new movie that I'll be filming," I say this as casually as possible, but I know I'm dropping a bomb.

"Wow, that's...surprising." Is all Santiago says, trying to sound as normal as possible, but there's an obvious shift in his tone.

"Why?" I broach, knowing that he's probably referring to the fact that I haven't mentioned anything about this yet.

"I guess I didn't realize you were already going to be filming something new, but also something that's across the globe. It's just a surprise to me." Santiago replies. His words and tone are so close to being normal, but I know that he's... frustrated? That's not the right word, but I'm not sure what else to use. Upset, maybe? I can understand where he's coming from, but I don't allow myself to let his opinion make me doubt my path, because I know this is the right thing to do. He's allowed to have his feelings, but I'm also allowed to feel proud of landing such an amazing role, and I can't feel guilty about it.

"Yeah, we talked about it a few months ago, but we made the final decision recently. I'm pretty excited." I respond, keeping my tone between neutral and excited. "From the research Marie has done on it, this should be a big hit."

"That's really amazing. I'm glad you're getting all of the opportunities you deserve." Santiago says, his tone genuine. "I'm proud of you."

"Really?" My voice is a little bit softer now, Santiago's words catching me off guard.

"Yes, of course. If I'm being honest, I'm sad that you'll be gone, but this is a good thing for you. A great thing." He says, amending the end.

"Thank you. I know I'm going to miss everyone here, but it should be just over winter break, so you won't even notice that I'm missing from school." My words are as comforting as I can make them, but I do mean them.

"Well, I'm going to miss you outside of school, too. You're important to me, and seeing you at school isn't enough." Santiago says, his tone teasing, his words anything but.

"Are you serious about that?" For a moment, I think I only internally asked that, but Santiago stops for a second, like he wasn't expecting the question.

"Yes, I really mean that. I know I *really* messed up in New York, but you've been so important to me these past few months, and I don't think there will ever be a world where you're not." Santiago confesses, the emotion in his voice raw and pure. "You've brought out a part of me that I didn't know existed." I meet Santiago's eyes, looking up into the mirrors of his soul, nothing but pure honesty in them. Biting my lip, I question whether or not I should tell him that he's really important to me, too. My earlier warning to not fall so hard so fast replays in my mind, and even though it hurts, I just squeeze his hand and nod.

"Thank you, Santiago." I must sound like the worst person on earth for that to be my response. If we continue like this, it won't be long before Santiago knows just how much he means to me. I need more time with him like this to just make sure that this is right. "You've been one of the most welcoming people here, and you've really been there for me." I see Santiago's eyes flicker, as though he was expecting something along those lines, but was hoping for more.

"So, tell me about this movie." Santiago says a moment later, once we've started walking again. His willingness to let me figure out my feelings while he's open with his is something I really appreciate, because it can't be easy to be the vulnerable one in a relationship like this. Whatever this is that we have, it's some sort of relationship, and we both know that. Santiago surely knows that I have feelings for him, but to what extent, hopefully, he hasn't figured that out yet. When I'm ready, I want to be the one to tell him.

I ramble off the parts of the plot I remember, and Santiago just nods and listens as we walk under the stars. The longer we're out, the colder I get, and Santiago eventually offers his jacket to me as soon as goosebumps appear on my exposed arms. Instantly, his smell is all around me, and I draw it close, breathing in the soft, comforting scent.

"Do you want to head back? It's getting late, and we

have school tomorrow." Santiago asks after we've done a full walk around of the pond, which is already quite a distance from the main building, where Santiago's car is parked.

"Well, I don't necessarily *want* to, but I think we should," I reply, not wanting the night to end.

We make it back to his car, and once we're inside the gates of my house, Santiago opens the car door for me, but neither of us make any movement to go our separate ways. Feeling more than impulsive, I reach up and place my hands on either side of Santiago's face, pulling his soft lips to mine.

If Santiago is surprised or flustered, I wouldn't know, because his hands are immediately wrapped around my waist as he pulls me closer. All thoughts of keeping my emotions in check fly out the window as we kiss, the tension between us crackling and shocking me. This is so much better than I remember. His hands on me, and my fingers wrapped around the hair at the base of his neck, tangling the soft strands over and over.

Santiago's hand moves to my jawline and brings me impossibly closer, a few of my curls pressing into his fingers. He slips the other hand up the side of my ribs and rests it between my exposed shoulder blades, the heat burning my skin.

Time passes by too quickly, and Santiago pulls away, his breathing ragged. He rests his hand on the side of my face, gazing deeply into my eyes as he catches his breath.

I chew my swollen lip, unsure of what to do now. That was the best kiss I've ever had, and I'm sure nothing will ever compare to it.

"I guess this is the time for me to escort you to your

door." Santiago finally says, sounding reluctant, but knowing that this is the end of our night.

"Probably," I whisper, slipping my hand into his as we walk up the path to my door. "Thank you for an amazing night. I had a wonderful time." Santiago smiles at this, his real, genuine smile.

"Thank *you* for giving me another chance." Santiago says, twisting his fingers around mine, before raising my hand to his mouth, allowing him to gently brush his ever-soft lips across the delicate skin there.

CHAPTER 35

Brooklynn

"Thank you so much for coming in today, especially on such short notice," Marie says, greeting me with a quick hug. "Hello, Mr. and Mrs. Carmine, thank you for accompanying Brooklynn. I'm so excited to say that you have officially been accepted for the Europe film, and you'll be flying out in early December." A large smile breaks out across my face, and both Mom and Dad wrap me in a hug.

"Congratulations, Honey," Dad says, pressing a quick kiss to my head.

"You're going to do amazing." Mom adds, gently squeezing my arm in excitement.

"The casting directors were more than thrilled when I told them that Brooklynn had accepted, and they were quick to let me know that you're officially a member of the crew," Marie adds, extending her hand for a high-five.

"That's amazing. I'm really excited." Is all I'm able to say, the shock still leaving my mind slightly dazed. Of course, I pretty much knew that this would be happening, but it's still exciting to hear the definite yes.

"This is an amazing movie, and I've already reviewed the script. Brooklynn, you're going to absolutely shine in this role. It's like this character was made for you to play."

Since my parents allowed me to skip the first half of school to meet Marie, they immediately drop me off for my last half after we leave. Luckily, I arrive between class periods, which means I don't have to enter a class that's already in session.

"Brooklynn, there you are! I missed you this morning." Carmen exclaims, reaching me with an exasperated look. "Seriously, school is boring without you. You're the only person I walk to class with."

"I'm glad I'm here to relieve you of your misery, then." I tease, linking my elbow with hers. "Have you seen your brother anywhere?" I blurt out, wanting to tell Santiago my news.

"Actually, I haven't seen him or Alessandro since this morning, but they can't be too far, since their next class is only down that hallway," Carmen responds, pulling me in the direction she pointed in.

"Hey, you two, look who decided to join school and be with us," Carmen calls out to Santiago and Alessandro, both of them turning their heads and immediately smiling. "Just so everyone knows, I had a pretty exciting morning, and there was good reason for me missing a few classes." I tease back, my breath catching slightly as I make eye contact with Santiago.

"Oh, and what would that be?" Santiago asks, wrapping his arm around my waist.

"I'm officially going to Europe in December for the new movie I'm going to be acting in." Carmen's jaw drops, and Santiago beams down at me.

"Seriously? That's so exciting!" Carmen gasps, pulling me into a hug. Santiago's arm remains around my waist, and she quickly lets go, a genuine smile on her face.

"I'm really happy for you, Brooklynn. You're going to do amazing." Santiago congratulates me, pulling me into a tight hug. He rests his head on my shoulder for a moment, pressing a quick kiss to my cheek before pulling away. "I'm so proud of you." I smile at his words, gazing into his eyes for a long moment before returning my attention to Carmen.

"Thank you, Carmen," I say, pulling her back in for a quick hug. "We need to get to class, right? I don't want to make us all late." I ask, knowing that I can't be bragging about my news, and also cause all of us to be late.

"Yeah, we should probably get going." Carmen agrees, glancing at the clock on the wall.

"Hey, wait. Do you want to go out later? As a celebration for you getting the part." Santiago asks, catching my wrist as I turn to leave.

"Yes, I do," I say with a smile, pressing my lips together in excitement. "Do you know what we're going to do?"

"Not yet, but by five I will. I'll call you later with the plans, and then we can set a time, if that's okay." Santiago admits sheepishly.

"That sounds perfect. I'll see you later then." I agree, turning with Carmen to speed walk to our class.

"I can't believe the person you've brought out in Santiago," Carmen comments as we walk. "He's like an old version of himself, but still the real Santiago, if that makes sense."

"Really?"

"Really. He really likes you." Carmen replies, nodding her head. "He's dated—I use that word loosely—other girls before, but he's never looked at them like he looks at you." I smile at this, the thought of being the only girl he's been like this with makes me happy.

"Sorry for being late, the traffic was kind of intense." Santiago apologizes profusely, opening his car door for me.

"Santiago, don't be silly. You're *five* minutes late." I say, reassuring him that I don't mind at all.

"I know, but I told you eight, and I meant it." Santiago replies, putting his car in reverse as he backs out of my driveway.

"Well, however long it was, you're here now, and that's all that matters." I finally say, mockingly rolling my eyes so that Santiago knows I really don't care. "What are we going to do at the beach?" I ask a few moments later, curious as to what exactly Santiago planned for us. All he'd said was that we'd be going to the beach, but not what the activity would be.

"I don't want to spoil all of my plans, but I will say that

it doesn't involve getting wet or anything, since it's getting colder at night." Santiago answers, glancing over with a smile. He used to barely smile when I met him, and if he did, it always looked rehearsed. Now, he's smiling more than he's not, and it's real. Noticing that about him reminds me of what Carmen told me earlier about him really liking me.

I really like him, too. I admit the words to myself, mulling the words over in my mind before realizing they're not true. I *love* Santiago.

I'm *in love* with Santiago.

The realization washes over my mind, and I turn to Santiago, taking him in as I allow myself to repeat the thought. I'm in love with Santiago.

"What?" Santiago asks, noticing my silent gaze.

"Nothing. I'll tell you later, once we're there." I say quickly. Now isn't the right time to tell him how I feel.

My eyes roam over every inch of him, all of the memories of us and our little ruse washing over me.

It feels like only minutes later that we're at the beach, even though I know that a decent amount of time has elapsed since we left. Santiago rounds the car and opens my door, helping me out before reaching into the back seat for a large, canvas bag that's bulging on every side. He takes my hand, and as we pass over one of the dunes, my breath is taken away by the moon and stars. There's not a cloud in sight, and it seems as though there are a billion times more stars than usual. Granted, I've only been here once, but this feels completely different. Impulse takes over me, and I tug Santiago's hand, pulling him behind me as we run down the dune, straight towards the ocean.

As soon as we've made it into the freezing, ankle-deep

water, I splash Santiago with the cold ocean spray, laughing at his fully amused face.

"Not so fast, now. Don't start something you can't win." Santiago says with a laugh, kicking up water of his own. Somewhere along the way, he must have dropped the bag, because his arms are completely free as he cups a large handful of water, sending it right at me.

"Cheater! I didn't use my hands!" I exclaim, using my hands to toss water right back at him. My splash lands directly on his face, and my mouth drops open. "Oops, maybe that was a little bit too high!" I say, feeling only slightly apologetic.

"Yeah, I'm sure." Santiago says, his words barely making it out before he begins uncontrollably laughing.

"What's so funny?" I tease, kicking a few more splashes of water on him while he's incapacitated.

"Oh, nothing," Santiago says, reaching down and cupping another big handful of water into his palms. "Just this." His water also goes directly to my head, but I turn, my hair taking the brunt of his attack. My hair is going to be so frizzy after this, but I can't bring myself to care. Whenever my hair is exposed to any humidity or salt water, it gains so much volume that it appears as though I have ten times more hair than I do.

We splash each other for a few more minutes before the cold really sets in, but pretty soon it's unbearably freezing in the water.

"It's a good thing I packed these," Santiago says as he reaches into his canvas bag, pulling out multiple large, fuzzy blankets. He lays one on the ground before wrapping me in another. Santiago pulls a different one around his shoulders, sitting next to me on the ground.

"Yeah, otherwise I might have insisted on going back to the car." I tease, scooting closer to him. We're so close that if we both weren't wrapped in giant blankets, the sides of our bodies would be pressed together.

"That wouldn't have been the worst outcome, although you would have derailed my plans a little bit," Santiago says with a laugh.

"Didn't I already do that when I splashed you with freezing ocean water?" I question, turning my head to face his. "Or were you going to ambush me?" Santiago gazes into my eyes for a moment before responding.

"No, it wasn't part of the plan." He says, moving his head even closer to mine. "But you make it sound like you premeditated that attack on me." I gasp, pushing him away slightly, as though I'm completely horrified.

"It was just a spur-of-the-moment idea. Don't worry, I don't have all of my attacks that poorly planned out. Usually they're *much* more concise." I say assuringly.

"I'm not sure whether or not I should be comforted by that, or if I should be worried." Santiago jokes. I lean back in, even closer than last time.

"Whichever you prefer," I whisper.

Our lips are so close that one breath would brush them against each other. Santiago's eyes drop to my mouth before bringing them back up to my eyes, and he drops his blanket from one arm, using his now-free hand to brush some of the curls that are framing my face back. He rests his hand on my jaw, using his finger to trail a line from my earlobe to my chin, going painfully slow, leaving my skin burning in its wake. I swallow, lightly biting my bottom lip as our eyes search each other's, ask if asking a question without even speaking a word.

As if deciding something, Santiago closes the gap between our mouths, firmly pressing his against mine, dropping the blanket from his other arm, using it to wrap around my blanket, pulling me impossibly closer.

I allow my blanket to drape from my shoulders, my arms free to slide up Santiago's well-defined shoulders, looping them at the base of his neck. My heart must be beating much faster than it ever has, the sound echoing throughout my body, drowning out the soft waves that land on the sand. The only sound I hear other than my own heart is Santiago.

Suddenly, loud, explosion-sounding noises ring through my ears, and I realize that the small town that's about a mile down the beach is setting off fireworks. "Was this a part of your plan? The fireworks going off?" I ask into his lips.

"Yes." Is all Santiago whispers back, drawing our mouths back together.

Both of our other kisses were passion-fueled, but this one has love at its center. Every touch and gasp from us is filled with a deep, intense love, and I don't ever want it to stop.

Just as I think this, Santiago pulls away, gasping for air, as though he's been swimming deep within the ocean, and he's just been pulled to the surface.

"We," he takes another breath, resting his forehead against mine. "We should probably stop." I don't like that I feel inclined to agree with him, but we were completely out of control, and it was the right thing for him to do.

"Probably," I whisper against his lips.

We wrap our blankets tightly around our shoulders again, lying back so that we can fully face the sky. The bright colors of the fireworks sparkle through the sky, leaving their glowing trails as more and more fireworks explode.

"Santiago, I want to tell you something." I say, moving my head so that it's resting on his broad shoulder.

"What?"

"I love you." My voice comes out clear, but there's deep emotion laced within it. Santiago completely stills, and even his breathing stops.

"You do?" He asks, as though he can't believe it.

"Yes."

"Brooklynn, I love you." Santiago suddenly sits up, a deep intensity in his eyes. "I've loved you for so long now, but convinced myself that you only thought of me as a friend."

"Really?" It's my turn to be speechless at his confession.

"When you first spoke to me, I was completely in shock, and knew that I wanted you to continue talking to me forever. And then every small moment after that just strengthened my feelings for you. When we were in New York and I kissed you, you left. I was terrified that you were going to tell me that everything was all for show, and that's why I didn't bring it up again." Santiago takes a breath, his words tumbling out too fast for even air to fit in. "Then, when I saw you that night, it was like my eyes were opened, and I knew that no matter what, I needed to do something. Whenever our eyes would meet for just a second, it felt like I was gazing into my future. My *future*. How does that even happen? How do you see your future in someone else's eyes? I didn't seem to know anything other than the fact that I need you more than I need oxygen. I need you more than I've ever needed anything in my life, and I wish I would have come to that realization much sooner. All I could think was, 'how have I gone this long without realizing she's it for me?'" Tears prickle at the edges of my eyes as Santiago speaks, every one of his words filled with emotion.

"Santiago, I love you." Saying these words again sounds so small compared to his confession, but I don't know when the moment clicked for me that I realized Santiago was it for me. Earlier in the car, it consciously clicked, but I know it was much earlier. Every moment when he was there for me and helped in any way possible, when he comforted me throughout some of the hardest moments of my life, and how he made me feel seen in a way that I've never felt before. All of that created a deep connection that I was too foolish to realize until much later, after I'd pushed him away. It took knowing what life was without him to know that I can never live in a world where I'm not his, and he's not mine.

"I love you, too, Brooklynn. So much. I promise to never make you question it again." Santiago's hand cups my chin and pulls my mouth to his, kissing me slowly.

CHAPTER 36

Brooklynn

"I'm really going to miss you," Carmen says, pressing her head on my shoulder as she hugs me tightly. She, Santiago, and Alessandro are all in my living room, giving me their goodbyes before my parents and I leave for the airport. Carmen has become like a sister to me in the last month, and while I think that dating her brother really adds a factor to it, I also know that she and I would have been friends either way.

"I'm going to miss you, too. I'll call you a lot." I say, squeezing her gently. "And I won't be gone for too long. I'll be back either right before or right after school starts again. Don't let any other girls try to hang out with you in between classes, because that's our thing." I tease, pulling away. Carmen laughs, smiling back at me.

"Don't worry, your best friend title will stay safe." She steps back, and Alessandro wraps his arm around her shoulder. I've gotten to know him pretty well, seeing as I'm best friends with his girlfriend, but also because he and

Santiago are just about as inseparable as Carmen and I are. According to Matteo—who I know somewhat well—they're as close as they used to be.

"Bye, Brooklynn. Get back soon, I don't want you to kill Carmen with your absence." Alessandro jokes, giving me a quick hug.

"I will. Make sure you keep her company since her favorite person will be gone." I tease, pushing him away from me, so that Santiago can pull me in for a hug. I vaguely hear Alessandro joke back with me, but his voice sounds far away as Santiago wraps me tightly in his arms.

Santiago's lips press against my throat, giving me a light kiss as he rests his chin on my shoulder.

"I'm going to miss you, but I'm also really happy for you. I'm almost happier for you than I am sad that you'll be gone." Santiago whispers into my neck, not loud enough for Carmen and Alessandro to hear.

"I'm going to be thinking about you the whole time I'm gone," I say, fully meaning it. I think about Santiago all of the time, but not being able to see him almost every day will definitely contribute to thinking about him a *lot* more.

"I'm going to be thinking about you, too." Santiago says. "But you can still call me even if it's the middle of the night over here. I'll answer."

"I will." I promise

"But you also need to have fun, too. You're going to be traveling all over Europe. This is going to be an amazing experience that you should try to take in."

"Are you ready to go? The driver is ready for us." Mom calls out. Santiago presses a quick kiss to my lips before pulling away, a smile on his face as he does so. I almost want to say no, but I smile back at him, calling back to Mom that I'm ready. Santiago says his goodbyes to my parents, and then he, Carmen, and Alessandro, climb into his car, waving at us before leaving.

I watch them for as long as I can see them, but after they disappear around a turn, I suck in a breath, slipping into the back seat of our car.

Whatever comes next, I know that Santiago and I will be okay, and no matter the time or distance, we're always going to be there for each other, and nothing will ever change that.

Epilogue

SANTIAGO

It feels as though there's a fire in my pocket, which is actively burning my leg. That's not true, of course, but that's the only way to describe how I feel. Patting the ring box that's securely slipped into my pocket, I run over my lines in my head once more. Brooklynn will enter the room, and as people wish her a happy birthday, she'll walk through the crowd, stopping right in front of me, waiting in the exact spot where we met four years ago.

It's time. Voices cheer as Brooklynn enters the room, and while I can't see her, I can feel her. She moves past a few people, and suddenly, she's right in front of me. Brooklynn's eyes are as beautiful as they were the day we met, and it almost feels as though no time has passed since then.

"Santiago?" She says my name almost quietly, like she's not sure what to make of the party, but also of my complete stillness. This is my cue! I should be on my knee right now!

Dropping my right knee to the hard, wooden floors, there's not a single noise around us. Focusing on only

Brooklynn's eyes, I swallow. "Brooklynn Chiara Carmine, would you do me the greatest honor of marrying me? When I first said *I love you* all of those years ago on the beach, I said that I saw my future in your eyes, and every day since then, I've seen it. I know that without you, there will be no brightness in my life. You bring so much joy into my life, and you awoke something in me when we met. You brought back a part of me I was sure would never be revived. I know what life feels like without you, and I never wish to feel that way again. Will you please marry me?" My words are raw with emotion and truth, and I've barely finished my speech before Brooklynn is saying yes.

"Yes, Santiago. I will marry you." Brooklynn's voice is clear, but tears are streaming down her cheeks. Extending her hand to me, I slip the diamond ring on her finger, the cut and size fitting her perfectly. I pull Brooklynn into a hug, and cheers erupt all around us as our friends and family celebrate us, but I don't pay them any attention.

"I can't wait to do life with you." I whisper into her ear, excitement rushing through my veins as I imagine us in five, ten, and twenty years. No matter how much our lives change, we're going to be together through it all, and nothing will ever change that.

I hope you enjoyed Rules and Reputations as much as I loved writing it! It would be amazing to hear your thoughts in a review on your favorite book retailers, review sites, and social media! You can find me on all social media platforms, as well as my newsletter.

- Jenevieve Hernandez

Acknowledgments

I would first like to thank YOU for picking up Rules and Reputations, as it means so much that you chose to read Santiago and Brooklynn's story! If this is your first Jenevieve Hernandez book, thank you! If you've read every Jenevieve Hernandez book, thank you! Every single person who has made it this far is so important, and I'm so grateful for you!

Thank you to my amazing family for supporting and growing my love for reading and writing from a very young age, and continuing to do so every single day. I wouldn't be here without you, and every day I'm so blessed to have you all.

Last, but definitely not least, thank you, God, for this gift You have placed within me!

- Jenevieve Hernandez

About the Author

Jenevieve Hernandez is the author of sweet and swoony romances, filled to the brim with the feeling of falling in love. She loves portraying character growth, unique plots, and, of course, romance in her books. Her books will never contain any explicit content, and are always guaranteed happily ever afters.

She enjoys spending her time in the pages of books, traveling from one story to the next, or outdoors, exploring the world around her.